The Rescuers

OTHER YEARLING BOOKS YOU WILL ENJOY:

With Illustrations By
Garth Williams

By Margery Sharp

THE
RESCUERS

A YEARLING BOOK

Published by
Dell Publishing Co., Inc.
1 Dag Hammarskjold Plaza
New York, New York 10017

Yearling ® TM 913705, Dell Publishing Co., Inc.
ISBN: 0-440-47378-0
Reprinted by arrangement with Little, Brown and Company.
Printed in the United States of America
Twenty-first Dell printing—September 1981

Contents

The Rescuers

1

The Meeting

LADIES and gentlemen," cried Madam Chairwoman
Mouse, "we now come to the most important item on our
autumn program! Pray silence for the Secretary!"

It was a full meeting of the Prisoners' Aid Society.
Everyone knows that the mice are the prisoner's friends
— sharing his dry bread crumbs even when they are not
hungry, allowing themselves to be taught all manner of
foolish tricks, such as no self-respecting mouse would
otherwise contemplate, in order to cheer his lonely hours;
what is less well known is how splendidly they are organ-
ized. Not a prison in any land but has its own national
branch of a wonderful, world-wide system. It is on rec-
ord that long, long ago a Norman mouse took ship all the
way to Turkey, to join a French sailor-boy locked up in
Constantinople! The Jean Fromage Medal was struck in
his honor.

The Secretary rose. Madam Chairwoman sat back in
her seat, which was made from beautifully polished walnut shells, and fixed her clever eyes on his graying back.
How she would have liked to put the matter to the meeting herself! An enterprise so difficult and dangerous!

Dear, faithful old comrade as the Secretary was, had he the necessary eloquence? But rules are rules.

She looked anxiously over the assembly, wondering which members would support her; there were at least a hundred mice present, seated in rows on neat matchbox benches. The Moot-house itself was a particularly fine one, a great empty wine cask, entered by the bung, whose splendid curving walls soared cathedral-like to the roof. Behind the speakers' platform hung an oil painting, richly framed, depicting the mouse in Aesop's fable in his heroic act of freeing a captive lion.

"Well, it's like this," began the Secretary. "You all know the Black Castle . . ."

Every mouse in the hall shuddered. The country they lived in was still barely civilized, a country of great gloomy mountains, enormous deserts, rivers like strangled seas. Even in its few towns, even here in the Capital, its prisons were grim enough. But the Black Castle!

It reared up, the Black Castle, from a cliff above the angriest river of all. Its dungeons were cut in the cliff itself — windowless. Even the bravest mouse, assigned to the Black Castle, trembled before its great, cruel, iron-fanged gate.

From a front seat up spoke a mouse almost as old and rheumatic as the Secretary himself. But he wore the Jean Fromage Medal.

"I know the Black Castle. Didn't I spend six weeks there?"

Around him rose cries of "Hear, hear!", "Splendid chap!", and other encouragements.

"And did no good there," continued the old hero gravely. "I say nothing of the personal danger — though what a cat that is of the Head Jailer's! — twice natural size, and four times as fierce! — I say only that a prisoner in the Black Castle, a prisoner down in the dungeons, not even a mouse can aid. Call me defeatist if you will — "

"No, no!" cried the mice behind.

" — but I speak from sad experience. I couldn't do anything for my prisoner at all. I couldn't even reach him. One can't *cheer* a prisoner in the Black Castle."

"But one can get him out," said Madam Chairwoman.

2

There was a stunned silence. In the first place, Madam Chairwoman shouldn't have interrupted; in the second, her proposal was so astounding, so revolutionary, no mouse could do more than gape.

"Mr. Secretary, forgive me," apologized Madam Chairwoman. "I was carried away by your eloquence."

"As rules seem to be going by the board, you may as well take over," said the Secretary grumpily.

Madam Chairwoman did so. There is nothing like breeding to give one confidence: she was descended in direct line from the senior of the Three Blind Mice. Calmly sleeking her whiskers —

"It's rather an unusual case," said Madam Chairwoman blandly. "The prisoner is a poet. You will all, I know, cast your minds back to the many poets who have written favorably of our race — *Her feet beneath her petticoat, like little mice stole in and out* — Suckling, the Englishman — what a charming compliment! Thus do not poets deserve specially well of us?"

"If he's a poet, why's he in jail?" demanded a suspicious voice.

Madam Chairwoman shrugged velvet shoulders.

"Perhaps he writes free verse," she suggested cunningly.

A stir of approval answered her. Mice are all for people being free, so that they too can be freed from their eternal task of cheering prisoners — so that they can stay snug at home, nibbling the family cheese, instead of sleeping out in damp straw on a diet of stale bread.

"I see you follow me," said Madam Chairwoman. "It *is* a special case. Therefore we will rescue him. I should tell you also that the prisoner is a Norwegian. — Don't ask me how he got here, really no one can answer for a poet! But obviously the first thing to do is to get in touch with a compatriot, and summon him here, so that he may communicate with the prisoner in their common tongue."

Two hundred ears pricked intelligently. All mice speak their own universal language, also that of the country they live in, but prisoners as a rule spoke only one.

"We therefore fetch a Norwegian mouse *here*," recapitulated Madam Chairwoman, "dispatch him to the Black Castle — "

"Stop a bit," said the Secretary.

Madam Chairwoman had to.

"No one more than I," said the Secretary, "admires Madam Chairwoman's spirit. But has she, in her feminine enthusiasm, considered the difficulties? Fetch a mouse from Norway — *in the first place!* — How long will *that* take, even if possible?"

"Remember Jean Fromage!" pleaded Madam Chairwoman.

"I do remember Jean Fromage. No mouse worthy of the name could ever forget him," agreed the Secretary. "But he had to be got in touch with first; and traveling isn't as easy as it used to be."

How quickly a public meeting is swayed! Now all Madam Chairwoman's eloquence was forgotten; there was a general murmur of assent.

"In the old days," continued the Secretary, "when every vehicle was horse-drawn, a mouse could cross half Europe really in luxury. How delightful it was, to get up into a well-appointed coach, make a snug little nest among the cushions, slip out at regular intervals to a nosebag! — Farm carts were even better; there one had room to stretch one's legs, and meals were simply continuous! Even railway carriages, of the old wooden sort, weren't too uncomfortable — "

"Now they make them of metal," put in a mouse at

the back. "Has any one here ever tried nibbling steel plate?"

"And at least trains were speedy," went on the Secretary. "Now, as our friend points out, they are practically impossible to get a seat in. As for motor cars, apart from the fact that they often carry dogs, in a motor car one always feels so conspicuous. A ship, you say? We are a hundred miles from the nearest port! Without a single mail coach or even private carriage on the roads, how long would it take, Madam Chairwoman, to cover a hundred miles in a succession of milk wagons?"

"As a matter of fact," said Madam Chairwoman blandly, "I was thinking of an airplane."

Every mouse in the hall gasped. An airplane! To travel by air was the dream of each one; but if trains were now difficult to board, an airplane was believed impossible!

"I was thinking," added Madam Chairwoman, "of Miss Bianca."

The mice gasped again.

3

Everyone knew who Miss Bianca was, but none had ever seen her.

What was *known* was that she was a white mouse belonging to the Ambassador's son, and lived in the schoolroom at the Embassy. Apart from that, there were the most fantastic rumors about her: for instance, that she lived in a Porcelain Pagoda; that she fed exclusively on cream cheese from a silver bonbon dish; that she wore a silver chain round her neck, and on Sundays a gold one. She was also said to be extremely beautiful, but affected to the last degree. —

"It has come to my knowledge," proceeded Madam Chairwoman, rather enjoying the sensation she had caused, "that the Ambassador has been transferred, and that in two days' time he will *leave for Norway by air!* The Boy of course travels with him, and with the Boy travels Miss Bianca — to be precise, in the Diplomatic Bag. No one on the plane is going to examine *that;* she enjoys diplomatic immunity. She is thus the very person to undertake our mission."

By this time the mice had had time to think. Several of them spoke at once.

"Yes, *but* — " they began.

"But what?" asked Madam Chairwoman sharply.

"You say, 'the very person,' " pronounced the Secretary, speaking for all. "But is that true? From all one hears, Miss Bianca has been bred up to complete luxury and idleness. Will she have the necessary courage, the necessary *nerve?* This Norwegian, whoever he is, won't know to get in touch with *her,* she will have to get in touch with *him.* Has she even the necessary *wits?* Brilliant as your plan undoubtedly is, I for one have the gravest doubts of its practicalness."

"That remains to be seen," said Madam Chairwoman. She had indeed some doubts herself; but she also had great faith in her own sex. In any case, she wasn't going to be led into argument. "Is there anyone," she called briskly, "from the Embassy here with us now?"

For a moment all waited; then there was a slight scuffling at the back as though someone who didn't want to was being urged by his friends to step forward, and finally a short, sturdy young mouse tramped up towards the platform. He looked rough but decent; no one was surprised to learn (in answer to Madam Chairwoman's questioning) that he worked in the pantry.

"I suppose you, Bernard, have never seen Miss Bianca either?" said Madam Chairwoman kindly.

"Not me," mumbled Bernard.

"But could you reach her?"

"I dare say," admitted Bernard — shuffling his big feet.

"Then reach her you must, and without delay," said Madam Chairwoman. "Present the compliments of the meeting, explain the situation, and bid her instantly seek out the bravest mouse in Norway, and dispatch him back here to the Moot-house."

Bernard shuffled his feet again.

"Suppose she doesn't want, ma'am?"

"Then you must persuade her, my dear boy," said Madam Chairwoman. "If necessary, bully her! — What's that you have on your chest?"

Bernard squinted self-consciously down. His fur was so thick and rough, the medal scarcely showed.

"The Tybalt Star, ma'am . . ."

"For Gallantry in Face of Cats," nodded Madam Chairwoman. "I believe I remember the incident . . . A cat nipped on the tail, was it not, thus permitting a nursing mother of six to regain her hole?"

"She was my sister-in-law," muttered Bernard, flushing.

"Then I can't believe you're not a match for Miss Bianca!" cried Madam Chairwoman.

4

With that (after several votes of thanks), the meeting broke up; and Bernard, feeling important but uneasy, set off back to the Embassy.

At least his route to the Boy's schoolroom presented no difficulties: there was a small service lift running di-

rectly up from the pantry itself, used to carry such light
refreshments as glasses of milk, chocolate biscuits, and
tea for the Boy's tutor. Bernard waited till half-past eight,
when the last glass of milk went up (hot), and went up
with it by clinging to one of the lift ropes. As soon as the
flap above opened he nipped out and slipped into the
nearest shadow to wait again. He waited a long, long
time; he heard the Boy put to bed in an adjoining room,
and a wonderful rustle of satin as the Boy's mother came
to kiss him good night. (Bernard was of course waiting
with his eyes shut; nothing draws attention to a mouse
like the gleam of his eyes.) Then at last all was still, and
forth he crept for a good look round.

In one respect at least rumor had not lied: there in an
angle of the great room, on a low stool nicely out of floor
drafts, stood a Porcelain Pagoda.

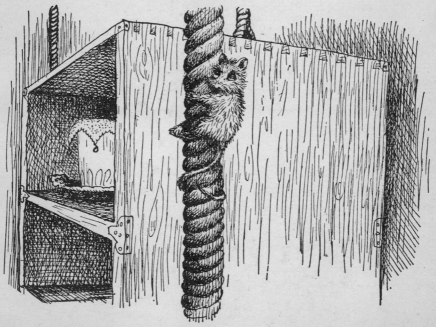

2

Miss Bianca

IT was the most exquisite residence Bernard had ever seen, or indeed could ever have imagined. Its smooth, gleaming walls were beautifully painted with all sorts of small flowers — violets, primroses and lilies of the valley — and the roof rose in tier upon tier of curly gilded eaves, from each corner of which hung a golden bell. Round about was a pleasure ground, rather like a big bird-cage, fenced and roofed with golden wires, and fitted with swings, seesaws and other means of gentle relaxation. Bernard's eyes felt as big as his ears as he diffidently approached — and he himself felt a very rough, plain mouse indeed.

"Miss Bianca!" he called softly.

From inside the Pagoda came the faintest of rustling sounds, like silk sheets being pulled over someone's head; but nobody appeared.

"Don't be afraid, Miss Bianca!" called Bernard. "I'm not burglars, I am Bernard from the Pantry with a most important message."

He waited again. One of the golden bells, as though a

moth had flown past, tinkled faintly. Then again there was a rustling, and at last Miss Bianca came out.

Her loveliness took Bernard's breath away. She was very small, but with a perfect figure, and her sleek, silvery-white coat had all the rich softness of ermine. But her chief point of beauty was her eyes. The eyes of most white mice are pink; Miss Bianca's were deep brown. In conjunction with her snowy head, they gave her the appearance of a powdered beauty of the court of Louis the Fifteenth.

Round her neck she wore a very fine silver chain.

Bernard took two steps back, then one forward, and politely pulled his whiskers.

"Are you calling?" asked Miss Bianca, in a very low, sweet voice.

"Well, I *was* — " began Bernard.

"How very nice!" exclaimed Miss Bianca. "If you wouldn't mind swinging on that bellpull, the gate will open. Are there any ladies with you?"

Bernard muttered something about Madam Chairwoman, but too hoarsely to be understood. Not that it mattered; Miss Bianca's beautiful manners smoothed all social embarrassment. As soon as he was inside she began to show him round, naming every painted flower on the porcelain walls, and inviting him to try for himself each swing and seesaw. "Pretty, isn't it?" she said modestly. "Though nothing, I believe, compared with Versailles . . . Would you care to see the fountain?"

Bernard nodded dumbly. As yet he hadn't even no-
ticed the fountain; it was in fact a staggering six inches
high, made of pink and green Venetian glass. Miss Bianca sat down on a hidden spring, and at once a jet of
water shot up out of the pink rosette on top. "There *is* a
way of making it *stay*," she explained, "but I'm afraid I
know nothing about machinery!" She rose, and the jet
subsided. Bernard would have liked to have a go himself, but he was only too conscious that time was passing,
and that as yet his message was undelivered.

Indeed it was hard to know where to begin. It was
such a jump from Venetian glass fountains to the Prisoners' Aid Society. Moreover, though he no longer
thought Miss Bianca affected, in fact he liked her very
much, he couldn't for the life of him see her doing anything more strenuous than swinging on a gilt swing. And
the turn the conversation next took fairly curled his
whiskers!

"I see you've been decorated," said Miss Bianca politely. (She was naturally familiar with medals, and orders, and ribbons.) "May I ask what is it for?"

"Gallantry in Face of Cats," muttered Bernard. —
First to his chagrin, then to his astonishment, she burst
into musical laughter.

"In face of *cats?* How very droll! I dote on cats!"
laughed Miss Bianca. "Or rather," she added sentimen-
tally, "on one particular cat . . . a most beautiful Persian, white as I am myself, belonging to the Boy's mother.

I used to play in his fur; I'm told we made rather a pretty picture . . . Alas, he is no more," sighed Miss Bianca, "but for his sake *all* cats will ever be dear to me!"

Bernard was absolutely speechless. He didn't disbelieve Miss Bianca; he could, just, imagine some pampered lapcat fat enough and drowsy enough to have lost all natural instincts; but what an appalling thought — a mouse going out into the world, alone, on a mission of danger, *not afraid of cats!*

"My poor playfellow! Ah me!" sighed Miss Bianca tenderly.

"Look here, you've got to promise — " began Bernard; and gave up. There was a dreamy look in her eyes which warned him, though he didn't know much about women, that it was the wrong moment to run cats down. Instead, he attempted to console her.

"You've got all this," he pointed out, looking round at the swings and the seesaws and the fountain.

"And what trifling it seems!" sighed Miss Bianca. "What trifling it must seem, especially, to *you,* compared with the real and earnest life of a Pantry!"

Bernard drew a deep breath. Now or never, he thought!

"Would *you* like to do something real and earnest too, Miss Bianca?"

She hesitated. Her lovely eyes were for a moment veiled. Then one small pink hand crept up to finger the silver chain.

"No," said Miss Bianca decidedly. "I'm so fond, you see, of the Boy. And *he* is so attached to *me*. How many times have I not heard him call me his only friend! I feel so, long as I do my duty to the Boy, my existence, however frivolous it may *appear,* is in fact quite earnest enough."

"That's one way of looking at it," said Bernard glumly. (They should have sent Madam Chairwoman, he thought, not him. Madam Chairwoman could talk about duty quite wonderfully.) "All the same," he persisted, "you're not with the Boy all the time. You're not with him now, for instance." (There was considerable point in this; it is at night that mice most want to be up and doing, and are most bored by inactivity.) "Actually, now that you've no longer your, h'm, playfellow, I really don't see how you occupy yourself."

"Well, as a matter of fact," said Miss Bianca modestly, "I write."

Bernard gaped. He had never met a writer before! — Though he was terribly afraid of wasting time, he couldn't help asking What.

"Poetry," confessed Miss Bianca.

How Bernard's heart leaped!

For so was the Norwegian prisoner a poet!

What a wonderful, fortunate coincidence! The very thing to make Miss Bianca change her mind! — Without giving himself time to think, and without any transition, Bernard blurted it all out — all about the Prisoners' Aid

Society, all about the great enterprise, all about Miss Bianca's part in it, all about everything.

The result was exactly what might have been expected. Miss Bianca fainted clean away.

2

Desperately Bernard slapped her hands, fanned her face, leaped to the hidden spring, turned on the fountain, with incredible agility leaped again and caught a drop of water before it subsided, sprinkled Miss Bianca's forehead. (Oh for Madam Chairwoman, he thought!) Seconds passed, a long minute, before the dark eyelashes fluttered and Miss Bianca came to.

"Where am I?" she murmured faintly.

"Here, in your own Porcelain Pagoda," reassured Bernard. "I am Bernard from the Pantry — "

"Go away!" shrieked Miss Bianca.

"If you'll only listen quietly — "

"I won't hear any more!" cried Miss Bianca. "I don't want anything to do with you! Go away, go away, go away!"

Greatly daring, Bernard caught both her hands and pressed them between his own. The action seemed to steady her. She stopped trembling.

"Dear, dearest Miss Bianca," said Bernard fervently, "if I could take your place, do you think I wouldn't? To spare you the least inconvenience, I'd walk into cat-baskets! But *I* can't travel by Diplomatic Bag, *I* can't get to Norway in twenty-four hours. Nor can anyone else. You, and you alone, can be this poor chap's savior."

At least she was listening, and at least she didn't push Bernard away. She even left her hands in his.

"And a poet!" went on Bernard. "Only consider, dear Miss Bianca — a poet like yourself! How can you bear to think of him, alone in a deep dark dungeon, when one word from you — "

"Is that really all?" whispered Miss Bianca. "Just one word?"

"Well, of course you've got to say it to the right mouse," admitted Bernard honestly. "And to find him I dare say you'll have to go into pretty rough quarters. I tell you my blood boils when I think of it — "

"Why?" whispered Miss Bianca. "Why does your blood boil?"

"Because you're so beautiful!" cried Bernard recklessly. "It's not fair to ask you to be brave as well! You should be protected and cherished and loved and honored, and I for my part ask nothing better than to lie down and let you walk on me!"

Miss Bianca rested her head lightly against his shoulder.

"You give me such a good opinion of myself," she said softly, "perhaps I could be brave as well . . ."

POEM BY MISS BIANCA, WRITTEN THAT NIGHT

> *Though timid beats the female heart,*
> *Tempered by only Cupid's fires,*
> *The touch of an heroic hand*
> *With unaccustomed bravery inspires.*

M. B.

3

In Norway

THREE days later, Miss Bianca was in Norway.

The journey, as usual, had given her not the least trouble. She traveled as always in the Diplomatic Bag, where she amused herself by reading secret documents while the great airplane flew smoothly and swiftly over mountain and forest, river, and, finally, sea. (To be accurate, there was a slight bumpiness over the mountain part, but Miss Bianca was too absorbed in a very Top Secret to notice.) Precisely twenty-four hours after departure she was reinstalled in her Porcelain Pagoda in the Boy's new schoolroom in Oslo, the capital of Norway.

It was then her mission really began; with, in Miss Bianca's opinion, far too much left to her own initiative. She was simply to seek out the bravest mouse in Norway! Without the slightest idea where he was to be found — or indeed where any mice were to be found! For Miss Bianca's life had been so remarkably sheltered, she really didn't know anything at all about how other mice lived. Except for Bernard, she had never even spoken to one.

Except for Bernard . . . Miss Bianca's thoughts flew to him so readily, she felt quite angry with herself. Now that the excitement of their midnight meeting was past, she couldn't help recognizing that good and brave as Bernard was, he was also completely undistinguished. — Yet how kind and resourceful, when she fainted! How understanding, when she came to, of all her doubts and fears! And how lost in admiration, how absolutely over-come, when she finally accepted her heroic task!

"I must be worthy," thought Miss Bianca. And mentally added — "Of the Prisoners' Aid Society."

So the very first night in her new quarters, she set out.

No one knew she was so slim that she could squeeze between the gilded palings of her pleasure ground. Certainly the Boy didn't know it. But she could.

The door of the new schoolroom didn't quite fit. In the morning no doubt someone would see to it; in the meantime, Miss Bianca slipped under. Outside immediately, she still felt pretty well at home — all Embassies being much of a muchness. There was first a broad corridor, then a broad landing, then a grand staircase leading down to a great grand entrance hall. (Miss Bianca, who had an eye for carpets, even recognized everywhere familiar patterns.) But she hadn't so far encountered any other mouse. "The Pantry!" thought Miss Bianca — remembering Bernard again. "But where on earth are pantries?"

However sheltered, all women have certain domestic instincts. Miss Bianca was pretty sure she ought to get lower down.

She also knew about service lifts. Passing from the entrance hall into the dining room, and observing a gap in its paneling (left open by a careless footman), up Miss Bianca ran to investigate. There inside, sure enough, were the proper ropes. "Obviously connected with the Pantry," thought Miss Bianca, climbing on. When after two or three minutes nothing happened, she boldly ran down — quite enjoying the easy exercise, and quite confident of finding herself in a pantry below.

Actually this particular service lift ran straight down to the Embassy cellars. Which was fortunate as it turned out, though Miss Bianca didn't immediately think so.

2

For what a sight, as she emerged, met her eyes!

Remember it was well after midnight, it must have been nearly two o'clock in the morning, the hour at which mice feel themselves most secure. In the Embassy cellar there was evidently some kind of bachelor party going on. At least fifty Norwegian mice were gathered there — singing and shouting and drinking beer. The most part wore sea boots and stocking caps; some had gold earrings in their ears, some a patch over one eye. A few had wooden legs. It was in fact the most piratical-looking party imaginable, and how any one of them ever got into an Embassy, Miss Bianca really couldn't imagine.

Never had she felt more uncomfortable. It is always trying to enter a room full of strangers — and *such* strangers! What a racket they made! The singing and shouting almost deafened her ears, there wasn't a moment of repose. (Miss Bianca had frequently assisted, from the Boy's pocket, at diplomatic soirees. *There*, always, was a moment of repose; in fact, sometimes the moments ran into each other and made *hours* of repose.) Even if she had shouted she couldn't have made herself heard, and Miss Bianca had never shouted in her life! She stood utterly at a loss, trembling with dismay; until at last a mouse nearby turned and saw her, and immediately uttered a long, low whistle. It was vulgar, but it did the trick. Head after head turned in Miss Bianca's direction; and so spectacular was her fair beauty, silence fell at last like refreshing dew.

"Forgive me for joining you uninvited," said Miss Bianca nervously, "but I am a delegate from the Prisoners' Aid Society, seeking the bravest mouse in Norway, on behalf of a Norwegian poet imprisoned in our parts."

Simply as she spoke, it was with a touching grace. Several mice at once cuffed one another for want of respect to the lady. Several tankards were kicked under benches. One of the soberest of the seafarers, who looked as though he might be a Petty Officer, stepped forward and touched his cap.

"Anyone from the Prisoners' Aid, ma'am," he said forthrightly, "finds all here ready and willing at the first tide. Just pick your chap, and he'll put himself under orders."

"How splendid!" said Miss Bianca, greatly encouraged. "Though how can I pick, stranger as I am? You must tell me who is the bravest."

"All of 'em," replied the Petty Officer. "All our lads are brave equally. Look about for yourself, ma'am, and count the Tybalt Stars!" (There was one on his own chest, with clasp.) "Some may look a bit rough to a lady — pipe down there, you by the bar! — but as to being brave, each and all rate A1 at Lloyd's."

Miss Bianca still felt any decision quite beyond her.

"Won't you choose for me?" she begged. "Of course it should really be a volunteer — but if you could give me any indication — "

The Petty Officer simply reached out a hand and clapped it on the nearest shoulder — only then looking around to see whom he'd got.

"You, Nils!" he snapped. "You a volunteer?"

"Aye, aye, sir," said Nils.

"Not a family man, or anything of that sort?"

"Not me," said Nils. (Several of his friends round the bar roared with laughter.)

"Willing to put yourself under this lady's orders?"

"Please, under the orders of the Prisoners' Aid Society!" cried Miss Bianca.

"All comes to the same thing," said the Petty Officer. "You just tell Nils what to do, ma'am, and Nils he will do it."

With that, as though no more had been settled than who was to run into the next room, all returned to singing and shouting and standing each other rounds of beer, and Nils and Miss Bianca were left alone.

She looked at him attentively. He was indeed rough to a degree. His sea boots smelled of tar, and his stocking cap had obviously never been washed since it was knitted. But he had good steady eyes, and he appeared quite unperturbed.

As simply as possible, Miss Bianca outlined the situation. She hoped he was taking it all in — he was so *very* unperturbed! — also he would keep humming softly under his breath.

"You're quite sure you understand?" she said anxiously. "How you travel in the first place I must leave to you — "

"Why, by ship — o' course," said Nils.

"I believe the Capital is some distance from the nearest port," warned Miss Bianca.

"Ship and dinghy, then," said Nils. "Wherever there's towns there's water — stands to reason — and wherever there's water, there us Norwegians can go."

"How resourceful you arc!" exclaimed Miss Bianca admiringly. "As to reaching the Black Castle itself, for that Madam Chairwoman will have a plan. You must get in touch with her immediately, at the Moot-house."

For the first time, Nils looked uneasy.

"Could you let me have a chart, ma'am? On shore I'm a bit apt to loose my bearings."

"Certainly," said Miss Bianca. "If you will give me the materials, I'll do it now."

After a little searching, Nils produced from one of his boots a paper bag and a stump of red chalk. (He found several other things first, such as half a pair of socks, a box of Elastoplast, a double six of dominoes, a ball of twine and a folding corkscrew.) Miss Bianca sat down at a table and smoothed the bag flat.

At the end of ten minutes, all she had produced was a sort of very complicated spider web.

The Moot-house was in the middle — *that* was quite clear; but the rest was just a muddle of criss-cross lines. Miss Bianca felt so ashamed, she rapidly sketched a lady's hat — just to show she really *could* draw — and began again.

"Hadn't you best start with the points of the compass, ma'am?" suggested Nils.

Miss Bianca, alas, had never even heard of compass points!

"*You* put them in," she said, turning the paper over. Nils took the chalk and marked top and bottom, then each side, with an *N*, an *S*, an *E* and a *W*. Then he gave

the chalk back, and Miss Bianca again put a dot in the middle for the Moot-house — and again, out of sheer nervousness, drew a lady's hat round it. (The garden-party sort, with a wide brim and a wreath of roses.) Nils studied it respectfully.

" *That* I'd call clear as daylight," he said. "You should ha' set your compass first." He laid a finger on one of the roses. "Them, I take it, would be duckponds?"

"Oh, dear!" thought Miss Bianca. She knew perfectly well where the Moot-house stood — Bernard had explained everything so clearly — but she just couldn't, it seemed, put her knowledge on paper. And here was good brave Nils preparing to set forth with no more guide than a garden-party hat!

"Yes," said Miss Bianca recklessly. "Those are duck-ponds . . ."

An idea was forming in her mind, an idea so extraordinary and thrilling, her heart at once began to beat faster.

"All the same," added Miss Bianca, "I think it will be wiser to return with you myself, and conduct you to the Moot-house in person."

What on earth induced her to make such a mad, unnecessary offer? Her own personal mission was creditably accomplished; no one expected any more of her; upstairs in the Boy's new schoolroom a luxurious Porcelain Pagoda waited for her to come back to it. As the Boy waited for her — or would wait, how anxiously, should she quit his side! Miss Bianca's eyes filled with tears as she thought of him. But she thought also of someone else: of Bernard from the Pantry.

It has often been remarked that women of rank, once their affections are engaged, can be completely reckless of the consequences. Duchesses throw their caps over the windmill for grooms, countesses for footmen: Miss Bianca, more discerningly, remembered Bernard's modesty and kindness and courage. "Did I call him undistinguished?" she chided herself. "Isn't the Tybalt Star distinction enough for anyone?" To make no bones about it, Miss Bianca suddenly felt that if she was never to see Bernard again, life in any number of Porcelain Pagodas would be but a hollow sham.

Thus, since obviously Bernard couldn't come to *her*,

it was she who had to rejoin Bernard; and fortunately duty and inclination coincided.

"Which I take very kindly," Nils was saying. "Can you be ready, ma'am, by the dawn tide?"

"What!" exclaimed Miss Bianca. Her thoughts hadn't carried her quite as far as that!

"It so happens there's a cargo boat," explained Nils. "Nothing like cargo boats for picking up a passage upon! And not so many bound your way neither — we should take the chance! In fact, in my opinion, we should start for the docks straight off."

"Heavens!" thought Miss Bianca. — Yet in one way it made her decision easier. The thought of seeing the Boy again, possibly for the last time — of running up onto his pillow and breathing a last farewell in his ear — was already almost unnerving her. "Better not," she thought. "I might break down . . ." She rose, smiling.

"Pray lead the way," said Miss Bianca. "I'm quite ready!"

They left at once. (Nils just fetched his cutlass from the cloakroom, and he was ready too.) No one bothered to say good-by to them, in fact no one took any notice of them at all.

"Do you always set out on a voyage so — so casually?" asked Miss Bianca, as they passed through the wood cellar. She really felt quite nettled.

"Stands to reason," said Nils. "Us Norwegians be forever setting out on voyages."

"But one so fraught with peril!" exclaimed Miss Bianca.

"All voyages be fraught with peril," said Nils matter-of-factly. " 'Drowned in his seaboots' you might call the national epitaph." He paused, and looked down at Miss Bianca's tiny feet. "By which same token, ma'am," he added, "where's your galoshes?"

"I'm afraid I haven't any," said Miss Bianca.

Nils gave her an odd glance, a glance she couldn't quite read. She felt nettled again.

"Traveling by Bag, as one usually does," she explained icily, "one doesn't need them. In Bag, one's feet are always quite beautifully warm . . ."

"In Norway, you're better with galoshes," said Nils. "You stay here a minute."

He hurried off, leaving Miss Bianca to wait beside a chopping block. (How thankful she was that no one she knew was likely to come by!) But he wasn't gone long; within a very few minutes back he came hurrying with a pair of lady's galoshes under one arm. " I've borrowed a pair of Ma's for you," he panted. — Miss Bianca looked at them ungratefully; they were far too large, and dreadfully shabby. However, there was nothing to do but to put them on, and she did so. "That's more like!" said Nils. "Now we can be on our way!"

Up they went by the wood chute, into the broad Karl Johans Gate. Nils ran straight across, and almost immediately entered a tangle of byways leading down to the docks. Slipslop in her horrid galoshes, Miss Bianca followed. "I'm not seeing much of Norway!" she thought. There was light enough, too, if they hadn't been in such a hurry; a strange pearly grayness filled the streets, all the house fronts were clearly visible. "Are we passing anything of historic interest?" panted Miss Bianca. But Nils wouldn't stop. He never stopped once until they reached the docks. There, bidding Miss Bianca wait again, he ran swiftly up and down reading the names on the vessels until he found the right hawser. "Follow me!" he finally cried; and Miss Bianca, by now completely out of breath, followed up into a very old, very shabby cargo boat.

4

The Voyage

OF the first part of the full month's voyage that ensued, Miss Bianca afterwards, and fortunately, remembered almost nothing. Most of the time she was seasick. Nils with the greatest kindness and practicality found her a snug berth behind the galley lockers — warm, dry, and, as you might say, next door to a restaurant; but though thankful to be dry and warm, Miss Bianca turned in loathing from even the excellent local cheese. A few drops of water, a few crumbs of dry bread, were all she could face. She lay curled on a bed of potato peelings — how different from her pink silk sheets! — and merely suffered. If the North Sea was terrible, the English Channel was worse — while as for the Bay of Biscay, Miss Bianca could never subsequently endure even to hear it named.

The spirits of Nils, on the other hand, as soon as they were fairly out to sea, rose and rose. He sang sea chanteys almost continually, often breaking out as well into snatches of a long saga about someone called Harald Fairhair. He ran in and out of scuppers, up and down the

rigging; there wasn't a cat or dog on board, reported
Nils joyfully — it might have been his own command!
"Come up and see!" he urged Miss Bianca. "Come up
and see the great billows, and how our vessel breasts
them! Come up and see the lights of the ports, how they
sparkle on the water! Come up and see the rays of the
great lighthouses — each and all specially designed for
the protection of us Norwegians!"

"I'm sorry, I have a headache," said Miss Bianca.

"A headache *at sea*? But the sea cures everything!"
cried Nils incredulously.

"I'm writing poetry," said Miss Bianca.

So indeed she was. She hoped that in the event of
shipwreck (which she fully expected), the following
lines, sealed up in an iodine bottle, might be washed
ashore and bring some comfort to the Boy.

POEM BY MISS BIANCA, WRITTEN AT SEA

Dear Boy! I would not have thee weep!
Sooner forget thy Miss Bianca quite!
Yet know, 'twas only Duty's higher call
Could e'er have torn her from thy loving side!

M. B.

The rhyme wasn't quite perfect, owing to seasickness, but it was the best she could do, and Nils kindly saw to heaving the bottle overboard.

He was as kind as possible — whenever he remembered her. It was a new experience to Miss Bianca not to be the center of attention, and led her to reflect a good deal on several points which she had hitherto taken for granted. Life in a Porcelain Pagoda had always seemed so natural to her! As cream cheese from a silver bonbon dish, and golden swings to swing on, and a silver chain to wear, seemed mere necessities! As she had told Bernard, Miss Bianca firmly believed that her devotion to the Boy made an ample return, and she believed so still; but it did not enter her mind that such an existence was unusual, and not the only possible one. Could one not find equal happiness, mused Miss Bianca, if not equal luxury, in devotion to another mouse? "Of course we should be very poor!" thought Miss Bianca. "I wonder how the poor live?"

She asked Nils. — She put it very delicately, in a roundabout way, so as not to hurt his feelings.

"What does your father do?" asked Miss Bianca.

Nils pulled his whiskers. — They were sitting together in the lee of a stanchion; it was a fine, calm night, very starry, and Miss Bianca had for once ventured up on deck.

"At a guess, he'll be voyaging — same as us," said Nils.

"But don't you *know?*" exclaimed Miss Bianca, astonished.

"Haven't seen the old buffer in years," said Nils casually.

"But who looks after your mother, and the family?" asked Miss Bianca. "How many brothers and sisters have you?"

Nils pulled his whiskers again. All mice have large families, and Nils was no better than any other man at keeping track of relations.

"A couple of dozen?" he suggested. "Soon as they're able, *they* go voyaging too — at least us boys do. The girls, until they marry, mostly stay home helping Ma. Ma takes in washing."

Miss Bianca shuddered. She had never imagined anything quite as dreadful as that! But she concealed her horror.

"No doubt it's because you're a race of seafarers," she said, "that your wives are left so much alone. Marrying a mouse in a good shore situation, such as a Pantry, for instance, would no doubt be very different. At least he would remain at one's side, in however modest a dwelling."

"As to that I couldn't say," replied Nils. "In Ma's opinion, the laundry runs a great deal better when she runs it herself."

"Poor soul!" thought Miss Bianca. Twenty-four children to support! — what deprivations *they* must have suffered! Perhaps not even new hats for Easter, and cream cheese only the rarest treat!

"How the poor live!" cried Miss Bianca uncontrollably. "It's quite dreadful to think of!"

"Is it? Myself, I don't know any poor," said Nils. He paused, and looked at her kindly. "Except, maybe," he added, "for one poor little female that hadn't any galoshes . . ."

Miss Bianca returned to her berth a thoughtful mouse indeed. She lay awake most of next day. To do her justice, Nils's silly misapprehension didn't occupy her long: Looked at in one way it was almost amusing — to own a Porcelain Pagoda, and yet be taken for poverty-stricken because one happened to borrow a pair of galoshes! (If only Nils *knew*, thought Miss Bianca, actually smiling.) No, what really engaged her attention was the fact that Nils didn't consider himself or his family poor. However small their income, he seemed to find it perfectly sufficient. Life outside a Porcelain

Pagoda was certainly *possible,* then, reflected Miss Bianca . . .

"But I could never, never take in washing!" she told herself.

With the best will in the world — and though she was rapidly shedding many of her prejudices — she couldn't believe Nils's mother to be *happy.* Alone all day at the mangle (except for say half a dozen daughters), and quite unsupported by a husband's company, how indeed could she be anything but wretched? — The picture would be very different, of course, with a loving husband in it as well . . .

"But I wonder if I could give drawing lessons?" mused Miss Bianca.

She was in a very distracted, uneasy state of mind; and to make matters worse, as the days passed and they began to near their destination, Nils started bothering her about the chart — a subject on which she was particularly sensitive.

Nils had taken charge of it at once, and kept it stowed in his left-leg sea boot, where it naturally rubbed against all the other things he kept there until it was quite smudged. Also the folding corkscrew must have come *un,* for there was a great round hole through one of the duckponds, or roses.

"*Really!*" exclaimed Miss Bianca, as he pulled it out. Secretly she was rather pleased; if *she* hadn't known how to draw a chart, Nils certainly didn't know how to take

care of one. "After all my trouble — !" exclaimed Miss
Bianca. Women can be dreadfully unfair, when prestige
is at stake.

"It looks all right to *me*," said Nils. "Why, Skipper's
chart up aloft you can't hardly read for cocoa! *I* can find
my way all right. All I was going to ask was, be they
duckponds linked by navigable streams?"

With growing horror, Miss Bianca realized that what
she'd intended for a map of the Capital, Nils took to be
a map of the route to the Capital from the port. In hon-
esty, she should have answered that she had simply no
idea — or have gone even further, and confessed that
the duckponds were in fact artificial roses. But what then
would become of Nils's confidence in her? It was dreadful to her to tell a lie; her only consolation was that she'd
practically told this one already, when she let Nils believe the roses to be duckponds in the first place, so it
wouldn't count twice.

"By navigable streams," said Miss Bianca.

"Simplifies things," said Nils happily.

"I'm sure I hope so," said Miss Bianca.

Nils took out the chart and studied it every day. He
liked studying charts. But poor Miss Bianca never
watched him without feelings of guilt and apprehension.

2

The days grew warmer and sunnier, the seas calmer.
They were in the Mediterranean. Miss Bianca, who had

done Greek and Latin with the Boy, spent more and more time on deck, gazing with a classical expression towards the fabled shores of Italy, Greece, and the Peloponnese. "Hector and the windy plains of Troy!" murmured Miss Bianca to herself. "The March of the Ten Thousand, the Spartans by the sea-wet strand, also foam-white Venus rising from the waves!" Never were the advantages of education better exemplified; she really forgot, for hours together, every distressing circumstance.

What she remembered was the Boy's schoolroom, in all its comfort and quietude; and the kindness of the Boy's tutor in allowing her to sit on the page; and the pleasure of shared intellectual achievement, as she and the Boy both got a verb right at the same moment, or memorized together some verse of splendid poetry. (Miss Bianca had had the best models.) In happy dreams, she saw Nils safe at the Moot-house while she herself ran back to the Embassy . . . She was quite confident that the new Ambassador would recognize her — if only by her silver chain — and take the promptest steps to return her to the Boy.

How she would enjoy traveling by Bag again!

It will be seen that Miss Bianca had once more changed her mind. Upon thinking it over she found she would prefer not to give drawing lessons. She was determined to bid Bernard but a last, fond farewell.

Two days later, they docked.

3

It is always agreeable to set foot on one's native shore again — and indeed Miss Bianca would have been glad to set foot on *any* shore; on the other hand, all seaports were equally foreign to her, and as she stood beside Nils on the quay (they had been among the first to disembark), she felt just as bewildered as upon the quayside in Norway. To make matters worse, it was now that her responsibility really began, and when Nils immediately suggested picking up a dinghy — obviously quite confident that she knew *where* one picked up dinghies — Miss Bianca could only pretend not to hear, for never was confidence more misplaced. She looked hopelessly about — up at the great hulls of the seafaring ships — up, even higher, at the great cranes unloading them — back towards the rows of customs sheds and warehouses — and really felt the situation quite beyond her. Then, fortunately, she looked down.

Bobbing against the foot of a flight of landing steps lay a model speedboat.

Miss Bianca could hardly believe her eyes. She recognized it at once. It was the Boy's, a gift to him from the American Naval Attaché — about fifteen inches long, and so wonderfully high-powered that the bathtub was scarred all round by its steely prow before some highhanded Someone indignantly fished it out. Then it had been lost. (Both the Boy and Miss Bianca suspected that

Someone of throwing it away.) And now there it lay, after what inconceivable journeyings by gutter, stream and canal, just as though dispatched by the Prisoners' Aid Society!

Miss Bianca instantly ran down, stepped on board and entered the cabin. What a relief it was to sit on proper cushions again! What a pleasure to see the elegant silver plating, the polished woodwork, the little bunch of artificial violets attached to a bulkhead! Even Nils, following, was impressed, as Miss Bianca welcomed him with the happy smile of the unexpectedly triumphant hostess.

"This is what I call organization," said Nils. "My word, she's a neat craft!"

"Custom-built," murmured Miss Bianca, "for a friend of mine. But do you know how to work it?" she added in some anxiety. "I believe it's what they call *atomic*."

"I was never yet aboard a craft I couldn't master," said Nils hardily. — Actually he pulled several wrong levers before he got the hang of things, and nearly swamped Miss Bianca in the process; but at last they were fairly under way.

What happened subsequently will be forever famous in naval annals. With a hundred miles to go, and navigating solely by Miss Bianca's sketch of a garden-party hat, Nils actually succeeded in reaching the Capital. If a duckpond, when he came to it, was bigger than he expected — actually a lake — Nils drove his vessel on regardless. There were navigable streams indeed, only they

happened to be rivers: Nils scorched up them like a motorist entered for the Grand Prix. Now and then he yelled back to Miss Bianca, over his shoulder, such exclamations as "Norway forever!", also his inevitable references to Harald Fairhair — but ever and always keeping an eye on the chart. (Miss Bianca, who naturally didn't recognize their course, could only hope for the best — but they were evidently getting *somewhere*, and far, far more comfortably than she had anticipated.) From time to time she fed Nils with coffee sugar out of one of the lockers. — Coffee sugar! How well she remembered the Boy stocking it, that locker, with his mother's specially imported coffee sugar! "How could I ever abandon him?" thought Miss Bianca, nibbling a pink bit herself. "Dear Boy, how could I ever think of abandoning you — ingrate that I am? As soon as I have dispatched Nils to the Moot-house, back, back to the Embassy will I run!"

With a final swish and swoop Nils rammed a familiar quay — one shallow marble step nudged by water lilies. The little lagoon in which they rocked was actually the Embassy's boating water. Almost overcome by relief and thankfulness, Miss Bianca emerged from the cabin and removed her galoshes.

"Correct landfall?" said Nils, switching off the headlights. (They had arrived about midnight, blazing like a rocket.)

"Perfect!" Miss Bianca congratulated him.

"Thanks to the clearest chart I ever steered by," said Nils. "Where to now?"

Miss Bianca swiftly reminded herself of Bernard's directions. The tavern in whose cellar the Moot-house was situated backed onto the Embassy stables — no more than a mouse-run away, across shaven lawn; and once inside the stables, there were signposts (as there always are in the vicinity of any historic monument.) Nils could easily find the Moot-house by himself, while *she* ran straight back to dear familiar surroundings . . .

But for several reasons Miss Bianca rejected this sensible course. One reason, it must be admitted, was that she wanted to get full credit for her heroism and be publicly thanked. If it was conceited, it was also very natural!

"Now we must report at the Moot-house," said Miss Bianca, "to which I will conduct you myself."

She left the galoshes behind in the speedboat. She nearly popped them overboard, but remembered in time they belonged to Nils's mother, who might want them back.

5

Marching Orders

ONCE again the Moot-house saw a full meeting of the Prisoners' Aid Society.

For the last week, indeed, members had been gathering there every night, in case the bravest mouse in Norway suddenly turned up. There were also some skeptics among them who believed he never would turn up, and who came simply to bait Madam Chairwoman. (The most mean-minded thing on earth is to rejoice in seeing a high endeavor fail; but it is not, alas, unknown.) The great majority, however, were decent, honest, well-intentioned folk, just eager to be in on any excitement going — and getting a little bored with waiting for it.

It can therefore be imagined what cheers burst forth when Nils and Miss Bianca, escorted by Madam Chairwoman and the Secretary, suddenly appeared on the platform!

"Cheer yourselves hoarse, my dear friends!" cried Madam Chairwoman triumphantly. "You have every reason to! Not only has this heroine —" she bowed towards Miss Bianca — "successfully accomplished her mission

— as witness the presence of our gallant Norwegian comrade — but she has even returned herself to be his guide! Hip, hip — "

"Hooray!" cried all the mice. "Three cheers for Miss Bianca! Speech, speech!"

Miss Bianca shook her head modestly. She just advanced towards the edge of the platform and bowed. Even so, the graceful way she did it aroused a fresh burst of enthusiasm.

"As for you, sir," continued Madam Chairwoman, turning to Nils, "your gallantry and devotion — "

"Think nothing of it, ma'am," said Nils stolidly.

" — will ever be illumined in the annals of our race! The Jean Fromage Medal — "

"That's right!" cried the mice from the floor. "The Jean Fromage! Give him the Jean Fromage! Give 'em both the Jean Fromage!"

"I was *going* to say," said Madam Chairwoman, "that the Jean Fromage, if this enterprise is brought to a successful conclusion, may well be eclipsed by the 'Nils and Miss Bianca'! Hip, hip — "

"Hooray!" cried everyone again.

Where in all this joyful pandemonium was Bernard?

He was sitting in his usual humble place at the back. He wasn't even cheering. He was too much overcome by seeing Miss Bianca again. Moreover, there was a thought he couldn't keep from darting through his mind: Was it *only* to guide Nils that she'd returned? Could it be just

possible that she had some other motive? As she advanced
in all her loveliness to the edge of the platform, hadn't
she appeared, however discreetly, to be *looking* for someone? Obviously she couldn't ask point-blank where that
someone was — female delicacy forbade; but supposing,
just supposing . . .

Bernard found himself tramping up on his big feet
towards the platform. He didn't care what other mice his
progress overturned — by now they were all out in the
gangways — he just needed to get as close to Miss Bianca
as possible.

"Thus you see how earnestly we thank you — " Madam
Chairwoman was saying to Nils.

"Miss Bianca!" whispered Bernard.

She glanced quickly round and ran to the platform's
edge. Across the row of potted plants, their whiskers
touched.

"Bernard!" breathed Miss Bianca.

"But you shall not attempt the Black Castle alone!"
cried Madam Chairwoman. (Bernard and Miss Bianca
must have missed a bit.) "I now call for a volunteer
to accompany and support our heroic Norwegian
friend!"

Instantly, simply to prove himself in the slightest degree worthy of Miss Bianca's regard —

"I'll go!" shouted Bernard.

Miss Bianca drew a deep breath. Admittedly such a
warmth of welcome — how different from the send-off in

Norway! — had gone a little to her head; but she was influenced even more by the look on Bernard's face.

"And I will too," said Miss Bianca — changing her mind again.

2

They received all last instructions in the committee room. (An old carriage lamp next door, tossed down into the wine cellar by a long-ago postilion. Generations of Prisoners' Aid Society members had made it extremely neat; in fact it was much more comfortable than the main hall, with walnut-shell chairs for everyone.)

"To pay compliments anew would be superfluous," said Madam Chairwoman briskly. "Therefore to business! You will travel by provision wagon. As you all know — or as we must inform our Norwegian friend — the Black Castle is provisioned but once a year. Once in each year, and only once, its gate opens to admit wagons from the country with flour, bacon, potatoes and so on. Thanks to Miss Bianca, we are just in time to catch them. They will halt at the Town Gate, to pick up cough-cure for the jailers, and there you must be ready tomorrow morning at five o'clock sharp. I believe the journey takes about two weeks; within two weeks," said Madam Chairwoman impressively, "you will all three *be inside!* The luck of the mice go with you! Any questions?"

Miss Bianca shook her head. She relied entirely on her

male companions. Nils, as usual, for his part seemed perfectly content to take whatever was coming as and when it came. Only Bernard spoke up.

"What do we do, *exactly*," asked Bernard in his painstaking way, "once we're *in*, to get the prisoner *out?*"

"That I leave to you," said Madam Chairwoman blandly. "I can't be expected to think of everything!"

3

It was next morning. Outside the Town Gate, in the soft, misty autumn dawn, the great cases of cough-cure stood ready for loading. (The Black Castle was so damp, its jailers had coughs all the year round.) And Nils and Bernard and Miss Bianca stood ready too. If they huddled rather close together, and if Miss Bianca's teeth chattered a little, it was probably because the dawn, besides being soft, was also rather chilly.

Nils had on his sea boots. Though Bernard thoroughly pointed out their uselessness, and indeed inconvenience, he wouldn't be parted from them. "It's no use arguing," said Nils. "Without my sea boots I wouldn't feel myself. That's how us Norwegians are." Miss Bianca smiled at him understandingly: she felt the same way about her silver chain. Bernard had pointed out the unsuitability of this too, he feared it might attract robbers; but without it Miss Bianca wouldn't have felt *her*self . . .

She carried only a small hand valise containing toilet

articles and a fan. (There had been little time for shop-
ping.) Bernard had a stout cudgel and an iron ration of
sealing wax tied up in a large spotted handkerchief.

"Hark!" exclaimed Miss Bianca.

There was a jingle of bells, and suddenly, out of the
dispersing mist, loomed an enormous wagon. Four great
horses pulled it, their heads bobbing and bowing somewhere up in the sky; and from far above even them, a loud
rough voice bellowed "Whoa!"

The wagon halted.

"All aboard!" cried Nils.

He ran swiftly up a trailing rope. Bernard seized Miss
Bianca's valise and helped her to follow. Scarcely had they
found shelter between two flour sacks when a series of
shuddering thumps told them the cough-cure was aboard
too; then came another loud shout, a whip cracked, and
off the wagon rolled, on its way to the Black Castle.

6

The Happy Journey

THEIRS was the leading wagon. Behind rolled five others. All six were loaded with flour, bacon, potatoes and black treacle, but the first carried in addition cough-cure, chewing gum and cigars. These last luxuries were for the jailers — the cough-cure for the common sort, the chewing gum and cigars for the Head. So loaded, and bound for so terrible a destination, it might have been expected that the journey would be terrible indeed, and Miss Bianca was prepared to cry herself to sleep every night, in the little tent Bernard arranged for her among the flour sacks.

But not a bit of it.

It wasn't impossible to be happy, it was impossible *not* to be happy — as the great wagons rolled and swayed on their way, bells jingling, harness glinting, under a strong October sun, through a countryside scarlet with turning leaves and gold with stubble fields. How tuneful those jingling bells, how bright each star and crescent winking from martingale and brow-band! — and the ribbons, too, plaited into mane and tail! Red and yellow and orange, the colors proper to autumn, how they enhanced a chestnut or dappled beauty! But best of all was the rhythm of the six great wagons rolling together, keeping distance yet ever in touch, like six great ships at sea. "Us should have sails set!" shouted Nils, running up the tailboard. "Five capital craft in line astern — and us aboard the Admiral's!"

It was astonishing how quickly the mice felt at home. They had the whole place to themselves, for the wagoner sat on his high seat in front and only once a day cast an eye over the load to make sure all was shipshape. They soon knew the names of their four horses, which were King, Prince, Emperor and Albert. Albert was Miss Bianca's favorite. (He had a very noble, serene expression. Miss Bianca was convinced, she told Bernard, that Albert had not exactly come down in the world, but had renounced the world. — She imagined him winning prize after prize at horse shows, before recognizing their vanity and humbly devoting his great strength to better things.) As to food, of course, no mice could have been better off: the whole wagon was simply one great running buffet!

That was by day; each night, all six wagons drew up in company, and the six jolly wagoners, after they had built a fire and eaten a great meal, told stories and sang songs. Not even Miss Bianca found their voices rough, then, as in beautiful deep harmony they begged their loved ones, also their favorite inns, never to forget them. (As one touching melody followed another, Miss Bianca's eyes were frequently wet with tears — really just as she'd expected them to be, though for different reasons. These were *enjoyable* tears — as the saddest songs were enjoyable to the jolly wagoners.) Each night she and Bernard and Nils slipped out of the wagon and crept closer and closer to listen, and if any item had the slightest rhythm of a sea chantey, Nils would join in; and afterwards they would all stroll back from the concert together, under the glorious moon. It was just like being at Salzburg.

Nils and Bernard had become very good friends. They hadn't much in common, but each saw that in whatever peril lay ahead, he could rely on the other's stanchness. — They never discussed this peril, or made any sort of plan for their great task of prisoner-rescuing. As Nils sensibly pointed out, it was no use crossing bridges till they came to them, and besides, they were having such a happy time, it seemed a pity to cast a shade over it.

2

Sometimes fieldmice came to visit, and then indeed was the peace of the wagon shattered. Whole villages swarmed up at a time — mothers and fathers, aunts and uncles, and of course the children — all chattering and arguing and gossiping and passing remarks. They never stopped asking questions, and never waited for an answer.

"Where are you bound, and why?" chattered the fieldmice. "My goodness, what a quantity of sacks! Unbelievable! Where do they all come from? And what's in those boxes? I say, Amelia, look at this fellow's boots! What's he wearing boots for? And look at the lady's necklace! My word! Look at this other fellow's feet, why isn't *he* wearing boots too? Couldn't he get any big enough? Ha, ha, ha!"

"Pay no attention," said Miss Bianca to Bernard. "They are only simple country folk, with no opportunity to learn manners." She didn't mean to be overheard, she spoke behind her fan, but fieldmice have very sharp hearing, and at once they all took umbrage.

"No manners, indeed!" they chorused. "Hear that, Amelia? The lady says we never learnt no manners! Hands up who goes to dancing class! Hands up all who know strawfoot from hayfoot! My word, she should see one of our barn dances! Come on, let's give one now!"

And they actually began dancing Sir Roger de Coverly there on the floor of the wagon — hands across, back-to-back, down-the-middle and all the rest. They *began* — but in half a minute they were all doing something else again: jumping on and off the cigar boxes, nibbling at the sacks, sliding down the treacle tins, and never for one moment ceasing their chatter.

"How strange! One always thinks of country folk as being rather stolid," said Miss Bianca. "I think I shall lie down a little . . ."

Bernard had found her a delightful veranda between two of the upright slats that formed the wagon's sides,

where she could rest in the afternoon and still look out at the changing landscape. It was considered Miss Bianca's private place, but she often invited the other two to share it, and Bernard at least never refused. (Nils preferred a spot higher up, on what he called the poop.) Miss Bianca and Bernard had many long conversations there, and told each other all about their past lives.

"What you must have seen," marveled Bernard, "of Courts, and Embassies! I'm afraid my society must seem very dull to you."

"Not at all," said Miss Bianca. "There is nothing more tedious than a constant round of gaiety. What *you* have to tell, of life in a Pantry, is far more interesting."

They talked in this way for hours, Miss Bianca describing things like musical evenings when the Embassy ballroom was decorated with six hundred pink roses, and Bernard describing things like Sports Day in the Pantry. (The biggest race twice round the top china shelf, five points penalty if you touched china.) They told each other their earliest recollections: Miss Bianca's of waking up on a pink silk pillow, and Bernard's of helping to roll home a walnut . . .

It was a happy time. By night songs and stories, by day agreeable conversation, and ever the beautiful landscape unfolding on either hand — it was a happy time indeed. If only it could have gone on forever! But the days passed, the wagons rolled, and presently the country began to change.

3

"The country's changing," said Bernard uneasily.

"Aye," said Nils. "We're out of the Mediterranean."

Miss Bianca at least knew what he meant. Bare heath and crooked firs, instead of fat farmland and scarlet maple — indeed they were approaching colder waters . . . She shivered a little, and put her fan away in her valise.

That was on the eighth day out; on the tenth, they entered The Barrens.

Here there were no trees at all, nor any sort of vegetation, only rocks and boulders strewing a great flat stony waste. The wagon trail still ran broad and plain, but the horses didn't like it; every mile or so they stopped and balked at something white under their hoofs, and the wagoners had to jump down and pull them past.

"What is it that alarms them so?" asked Miss Bianca curiously.

Bernard didn't want to tell her, but she persisted and he had to. "Bones," said Bernard grimly. "The bones of the prisoners who died on the march to the Black Castle."

Miss Bianca shuddered, and asked no more. Some of the bones had fetters still upon them, for as a prisoner fell so he was left to lie. Then the crows came down and picked him clean.

Albert was the bravest horse, but even he trembled all over. His bells trembled too, not jingling any more, but giving out a faint, mournful, funereal chime.

The fieldmice had vanished long since. In The Barrens, there was no life at all.

At night, the wagoners sounded like people singing to keep their spirits up. Nils and Bernard and Miss Bianca stayed in the wagon.

On the twelfth day, the trail began to climb. The boulders closed their ranks until it was like driving between rocky walls, and then between rocky bluffs, and then between great cliffs. High as the trail climbed, these cliffs rose ever higher, beetling overhead like storm clouds made solid; and here the bones lay thicker.

This lasted for two days more.

On the fourteenth day, quite suddenly, the summit was reached, and all dropped away before the one highest peak of all, which was the Black Castle itself.

They had arrived.

As though the very mountain split, an enormous iron gate swung slowly open, and the wagons rolled through.

7

The Black Castle

Iт was an appalling moment, and an appalling place.

Behind them was the huge buttressed gateway; on all other three sides of the courtyard great grim black walls, windowless, reared up quite out of sight. There wasn't a scrap of creeper or greenery upon them. Between the paving stones underfoot not so much as a toadstool sprouted. All was iron-hard, iron-chill, and black as old iron.

The air was like the air in a well. Not so very high up in it, a few carrion crows silently hovered.

In silence, as though the Black Castle awed even them, the wagoners began to unload their wagons; there was no need for orders or instructions, they had done the job before, and were only too anxious to get it over. The kind horses nickered and whinnied uneasily; but no human sound was to be heard save the coughing of the jailers waiting to get at the cases of cough-cure.

"What do we do now?" whispered Miss Bianca. The three mice had run down at once, and were now huddled together beside a wheel.

"Wait, then follow the best boots," muttered Nils.

There were boots stamping and shifting all round them — great cruel jailers' boots, black as everything else in the Black Castle. Even Bernard turned a trifle pale, but he nodded bravely.

"You be leader," he whispered.

They waited for what seemed like hours — Nils meanwhile scrutinizing attentively each pair of feet that passed. All seamen have an eye for a boot; and even though these weren't the sort he was used to, he had soon made up his mind. When at last the wagons filed out again, and the jailers began to disperse —

"Follow me!" cried Nils unhesitatingly.

Miss Bianca cast one longing farewell glance towards the tailboard of the last wagon. Even as it passed the gate, sunlight seemed once more to fall upon it; the wagoners were already calling and shouting to each other again, as they headed back into the jovial, sunlit countryside. How glad they were to be going! "And how glad *I* should be!" thought poor Miss Bianca.

She very nearly ran after them. The gates weren't yet quite closed. By running as fast as she could, she might have just caught up; and have run up on board again, and been carried back to safety and civilization . . .

"Miss Bianca," called Bernard urgently, "do please hurry!"

She sighed; and followed duty's higher call.

2

"See any hole?" muttered Nils.

"There, by the stove," whispered Bernard. (He was much cleverer than Nils *indoors.*) "Run in quick, Miss Bianca!"

A moment later they were all looking out, from at least temporary security, upon the Head Jailer's private sitting room.

For that was where the best boots had led, before stamping out again — and how luckily! What Bernard had spotted was actually *the only mousehole in the Black Castle.* The walls of no single other apartment were wainscoted. From the dungeons below to the battlements above, all was either natural rock or bare granite blocks. (Even the jailers' bedrooms weren't so much as white-washed.) As yet, of course, the mice didn't realize their good fortune; they barely glanced at the quarters they were in future to know so well, before examining the larger quarters outside.

"Oh, how *pretty!*" breathed Miss Bianca in surprise.

At first glance, the Head Jailer's sitting room was pretty indeed. The upper part of each wall, above the wainscot, appeared to be hung with the most charming varicolored paper — all reds and blues and browns and yellows. "Just like butterflies!" added Miss Bianca admiringly. — Then she shuddered. For when one looked closer, they *were* butterflies, each cruelly impaled by a lethal pin. Very many, as their poor broken wings showed, hadn't even died in a killing-bottle. And they covered half of every wall! The Head Jailer must have been collecting them, and tormenting them, for years and years . . .

He had evidently other horrid habits as well. Strewn all about the floor were cigar butts and the wrappers off packets of chewing gum: as though he couldn't live without something in his mouth, and hadn't been brought up to tidy as he went along.

"I'm so sorry, but really I feel quite faint," said Miss Bianca.

"Go and lie down a bit," said Bernard kindly. "It looks quite clean inside. — At least he's shortsighted, don't you think?" he added to Nils, as Miss Bianca thankfully withdrew. "He didn't notice us under his heels?"

"He's too fat to see past his own stomach," said Nils crudely. "So far as *he's* concerned, I'd say we could run where we liked. But it's to be hoped he doesn't keep a cat . . ."

The words woke in Bernard a most uncomfortable recollection . . . of an old, old member, at that meeting of the Prisoners' Aid Society when everything started. Hadn't he referred, quite positively, to the Head Jailer's cat? *"Twice natural size, and four times as fierce"* — Bernard recollected the very phrase.

"He keeps a cat all right," said Bernard gloomily.

At that very moment — for the Head Jailer liked to leave his own door open — Mamelouk lounged into the room.

With splendid presence of mind Bernard yanked a

cigar butt across the entrance to the hole, thus masking all mouse scent, and above this malodorous barricade he and Nils peered anxiously out.

The cat Mamelouk yawned, stretched, and finally leaped up into the Head Jailer's armchair. He was an enormous black half-Persian, with a coat like a thundercloud and eyes like dirty emeralds. When veiled, they were menacing; when wide open, hypnotic. Even for a cat, his self-assurance was staggering. With the Head Jailer under his thumb, he was King of the Black Castle, and well he knew it.

"Nasty customer, eh?" muttered Nils.

"We must keep Miss Bianca out of his way," said Bernard.

"No more than a couple of mouthfuls," agreed Nils, "*she*'d make for him . . ."

It crossed their minds that neither of *them* would make more than a couple of mouthfuls either. They watched Mamelouk in silence for a few minutes longer, and then thoughtfully rejoined Miss Bianca, and warned her that she was never, in any circumstances, to go out of the hole alone.

3

The hole was their home.

It had several disadvantages. Mamelouk was always liable to turn up in the sitting room outside, and the necessary smell of cigar butts at the entrance made Miss Bianca almost ill. But when Nils and Bernard, after several daring reconnaissances, discovered that there was absolutely no other accommodation available, they sensibly made the best of it, and at least it was a splendid listening post.

They made it really very nice.

The entrance passage, which ran directly at right angles from the wainscot, was quite two and a half inches long, and this was their lobby, where were kept Bernard's cudgel, Nils's sea boots and cutlass, and Miss Bianca's valise. (It was essential to be tidy; and they had the Head Jailer's awful example.) Beyond, between the wainscot and the original granite, and from the stove to the outer wall, stretched a quite commodious apartment. Bernard cleverly divided it with match-boarding — the sitting room floor was quite littered with empty matchboxes — to make Miss Bianca a bedroom by the stove, a slightly larger one for himself and Nils at the other end, and a parlor for general use in between. There Miss Bianca took charge. She had always had a taste for interior decoration, and the lack of professional assistance but sharpened her wits. Soon gay chewing-gum wrappers papered the walls, while upon the floor used postage stamps, nibbled off envelopes in the Head Jailer's wastebasket, formed a homely but not unsuitable patchwork carpet. Miss Bianca with her own hands fashioned several flower pieces — so essential to gracious living — from bread crumbs dyed pink or blue with red or blue-black ink.

At least they had no need to economize where food was concerned: the Head Jailer had all his meals sent up on trays, and was a very untidy eater. Miss Bianca even made one or two daffodils out of cheese.

All heavy work was of course done by Nils and Bernard — the carpentry and paperhanging and so on; Miss Bianca just had the ideas.

Naturally such an amount of work took time, but it was well they were kept busy, otherwise their spirits might have sunk unendurably low.

4

As it was, they sank low enough.

One of the mice's first acts had of course been to constitute themselves into a subsection of the Prisoners' Aid Society, Black Castle Branch. Nils and Bernard voted Miss Bianca Madam Chairwoman, Bernard was Secretary, and they held a General Meeting once a week. As meeting succeeded meeting, however, these grew shorter and shorter and gloomier and gloomier; for the more information the mice gathered, the more hopeless their mission appeared.

As witness the following digest of several earlier Minutes:

Each prisoner occupied a separate dungeon deep down in the rock, and these dungeons were never opened. Food (black bread and treacle) was let down, but once a day, each morning, through grids in the ceilings; and these grids were set in the floor of a long stone corridor itself cut off from the rest of the Castle by a locked iron door.

(SOURCE: Instructions from Head Jailer to new common sort of jailer, in H.J.'s sitting room: overheard by all Members.)

(QUERY: How were the prisoners got *into* their dungeons? The Members couldn't think.)

The door fitted too closely for even a mouse to run under.

(SOURCE: Nils.)

Once a day, of course, it was unlocked by the jailer with the food pans, and then Nils was pretty certain he could have got in too — if it hadn't been for Mamelouk the cat, see below.

Mamelouk regularly accompanied the jailer on his rounds. It was his horrible amusement to jump down into a dungeon, as soon as the grid was opened, and torment the prisoner by spitting at him while he ate, and then ride up again on the food pan.

(SOURCE: Gossip of jailers: overheard by Nils and Bernard.)

(MINORITY OPINION: Perhaps Mamelouk was trying to *cheer* the prisoners? — M. B.)

The jailer mightn't notice Nils, but Mamelouk certainly would.

"One of these days I'll risk it all the same!" cried Nils desperately. "I'm no nearer getting in touch with the poor chap than if I'd never left Norway!"

"Don't be an idiot," said Bernard, "you wouldn't stand a chance. There can't be an inch of cover down there: it's just one big trap."

As the whole Castle was an even bigger trap.

Except for the great gate, there was no way out at all. The wagons had approached from the south: on the northern side, it was as though the mountain range had been sliced clean away; the Castle rose straight up from the very verge of a tremendous cliff. Below flowed the River, bridgeless as far as eye could see, and on the farther bank stretched the same sort of country as The Barrens. No wonder *that* side was never guarded! But indeed there seemed as little reason for the jailers in the watchtower above the gate . . .

"Even suppose we could rescue him from his dungeon," said Bernard gloomily — "him" always meant the Norwegian prisoner — "how on earth would we get him *out?*"

This particular conversation took place not at a meeting but in the parlor, where they were all sitting round a fire of cedarwood. (Cigar boxes burn beautifully.) The leaping flames made it look very cozy, playing over the fresh wallpaper and the gay carpet and Miss Bianca's flower pieces. No amount of physical comfort, however, can lighten the burden of responsibility to a truly conscientious mind.

"Cross *that* bridge when we come to it," said Nils shortly.

"You mean you can't think of anything," said Bernard. "I'm not blaming you; *I* can't either."

"What troubles *me* — " began Miss Bianca. She hesitated. What was in her mind was something so dreadful, she felt she really ought to keep it to herself. Then she felt she really couldn't. "What troubles *me,*" whispered Miss Bianca, "is that we don't *know* . . . we have no means of knowing . . . whether he's even still *alive!*"

She looked anxiously at Nils and Bernard; they were looking at each other.

"We hoped you wouldn't think of it," said Bernard reluctantly.

"You mean you and Nils *have?*"

Nils nodded. "Stands to reason," he said gravely. "Put *me* in a dungeon, I wouldn't last a week!"

"But we won't give up hope," said Bernard quickly. "We don't *know* one way or the other. Remember the luck of the mice!" he added cheerfully. "Hasn't it brought us all the way here — found us this splendid hole — kept us all fighting-fit and ready for anything? Remember how beastly we thought the wagon ride was going to be, and how jolly it turned out! And you, Nils, remember that chap Harald Fairhair you're always singing about, remember 'Up the Norwegians!' "

Nils reached across and grasped him by the hand; Miss Bianca slipped hers into his other. Whate'er befell, at least they were three united, loyal companions. At the moment, it was their only consolation.

POEM BY MISS BIANCA, WRITTEN IN THE BLACK CASTLE

Black as the Castle press my mournful thoughts!
What ray of hope can e'er their gloom dispel?
Again, dear Boy, your Miss Bianca fond
Bids you a last, an ultimate farewell!

M. B.

Actually this was the most depressing poem she ever wrote, but even at the time, because it so exactly expressed her feelings, she was rather cheered up by it. Poets have uncommon advantages — as will be seen later on.

8

Waiting

THE pleasantest place in the Black Castle — or rather the least depressing — was a little stone ledge outside the Head Jailer's window. It wasn't a proper window sill, it couldn't have taken a flowerpot, but it was wide enough for a mouse to sit on, in the fresh air. Every afternoon, before setting out on his rounds, the Head Jailer used to raise the sash a couple of inches — his was the only window in the Castle without bars — and as soon as his back was turned Nils and Bernard and Miss Bianca used to run up and sit outside. It was really quite nice, though one of them had always to keep watch for the Head Jailer's return; he closed the window again immediately. Like most wicked people, he hated fresh air; this was the only airing his room ever got. So the three mice had to be careful to regain their hole in time, otherwise they would have had to make a long, dangerous journey round by a corridor window and back through the sitting room door. Nils and Bernard took turns watching — they took fair turns at everything — while the others looked at the view. In time it grew very, very familiar.

Far below ran the great River — sometimes angry, sometimes smooth: and when it was smooth huge rafts floated by, so stacked with logs they looked like floating woodpiles. In the stern of each was built a sort of hut or shelter made of reeds, for the raft-men to sleep in; and if there was a raft-woman — a raft-wife — aboard, there would be hens and hencoops as well, and most likely washing out. When it was rough, they evidently tied up somewhere along the banks, for then not a craft was to be seen, and when they reappeared it was in bunches of six or seven at a time.

"Where can they all be going?" marveled Miss Bianca.

"Why, to the towns, o' course," said Nils, "with winter firing. Don't you use firewood in these parts?"

"At the Embassy, we used central heating," said Miss Bianca.

Nils laughed loudly.

"And where d'you suppose the heat comes from?"

"You forget," said Bernard quickly, "that Miss Bianca has never had to occupy herself with housekeeping. In these parts, as you call them, ladies don't."

Miss Bianca threw him a grateful look. But she was very anxious there should be no bickering. Tempers fray so easily, when one is anxious and frustrated!

"Nils can never get used to my incompetence," said she gently. "But it didn't stop him being very kind to me, on shipboard!"

As a matter of fact, and to their great credit, their

bickerings were very rare, and never lasted more than a few moments. Just a touch of crossness, now and again, was inevitable, for they were frustrated and anxious indeed. The thought of the poor prisoner was never far from their minds, and yet their anxiety to be *doing* something for him was coupled with such a complete inability to think *what*. Bernard relieved himself a little by digs at Madam Chairwoman (not of course referring to Miss Bianca); whenever Nils made his remark about crossing bridges — "I'd like to see Madam Chairwoman cross *this* one!" Bernard would mutter bitterly; that absent figure became really quite a useful scapegoat. Very much, however, was due to Miss Bianca, whose perfect manners and unfailing *savoir-faire* would have soothed the tempers of tigers.

Which was all the more creditable to *her,* since she in one respect was having the worst of things. By day, the three mice could support each other's spirits; Bernard and Nils, sharing a room, could talk to each other at night too. Poor Miss Bianca was all alone.

Quite often she got up, and crept into the parlor, just to hear the sound of their voices. Although the things they talked about weren't particularly cheerful!

"*I* wouldn't last a week," she heard Nils mutter sleepily. "Not in a dungeon I wouldn't . . ."

"I'd last a month," mumbled Bernard. "I'd last two months . . ."

Nils evidently woke up.

"Bet you you wouldn't!"

Bernard woke up too.

"Bet you I would!"

"Bet you a double six of dominoes," said Nils, "you'd be dead and gone, and carried out feet first, inside *ONE WEEK.*"

"And *I* bet *you*," countered Bernard, "two potatoes and a walnut, that I'd still be there to shout 'Up the Norwegians!' as they shoveled you under — having still *ONE MONTH AND THREE WEEKS TO GO.*"

"I take you," said Nils.

"And *I* take *you*," said Bernard.

There was a slight pause.

"Who's to hold the stakes?"

"Miss Bianca."

Miss Bianca shuddered. — But in the morning, neither Nils nor Bernard said a word about it, and with a mixture of relief and irritation she concluded that they had just been playing a masculine game, like golf.

She still envied them. And how she envied them even more, when the thunderstorms began!

Each year, it seemed, as winter approached, such unnatural storms buffeted the Castle unceasingly. All too soon the pattern became familiar: first an ominous stillness in the air, as though presaging snow — not a sound in all the Castle save the coughing of the jailers — then a little stir of wind, the storm's outrider, then the first lightning flash, and then — crash! — instead of snow the thunderbolts, banging like artillery fire against the Castle walls. From watchtower to dungeons the whole place shook; and Miss Bianca, in bed, put her head under her pillow. Or else she got up and sat in the parlor — and once at least met Bernard, coming to see if she was all right.

"Are you all right, Miss Bianca?" asked Bernard anxiously.

Miss Bianca pulled herself together.

"Thunderstorms always have played havoc with my nerves!" she apologized. "Even under the Boy's pillow, they used to set me quaking! — Actually I just came to see that the fire was out."

Bernard kicked at the hearth, and said yes it was, at least there was no danger from fire.

"Then I'll go back to bed," said Miss Bianca bravely. She paused a moment, however, and heaved a little sigh. "Oh, Bernard," she added wistfully, "how long ago it seems, that night we first met, in my beautiful, safe Porcelain Pagoda!"

2

Indeed it seemed long; and indeed it *was* long — from full summer until almost midwinter. First there had been Miss Bianca's air trip to Norway, then the long voyage back, then the wagon journey, and now nearly two months in the Black Castle. And without achieving anything! That was the hardest to bear of all. "If only something would *happen!*" they began to think . . .

Something did.

They had been in the Black Castle exactly two months and a day, when a most terrible event occurred.

Bernard was sitting on the Ledge alone. Miss Bianca had one of her headaches, and since they never left her by herself, Nils was staying indoors too. It was his turn. Bernard would have been the one gladly, but in any situation of danger it is always best to keep strictly to rules. — Imagine his amazement, therefore, to wake from a light doze and see Nils coolly seated beside him!

"Don't worry," said Nils easily. "Miss Bianca didn't want me, so I thought I'd join you for a breath of air. She *can,* you know, be just a bit of a nuisance!"

Bernard was so horrified, he nearly fell off the Ledge. "But suppose Mamelouk comes in?" he cried.

"Even if he does — " began Nils.

At that very moment, Mamelouk appeared inside.

Bernard dashed towards the window — too late! In *that* very moment, an old sash cord irretrievably frayed, and down the window slammed.

"Looks like we'll have to take the long passage round," said Nils, still unperturbed.

"And what about Miss Bianca?" shouted Bernard. "Alone in there with Mamelouk?"

"She's only to keep safe in the hole," said Nils reasonably. "Stands to reason, she won't venture out — "

Bernard caught him by the scruff and shook him till his teeth rattled.

"You idiot!" he shouted. "You irresponsible idiot! Not venture out! Don't you know that Miss Bianca *isn't afraid of cats?*"

They stared at each other in horror.

"Come quick!" gasped Bernard. "We can do nothing here — and I couldn't bear," he sobbed, "to *watch!*"

9

Cat-and-Mouse

His fears were only too well founded. Scarcely had he and Nils rushed from the Ledge, when Miss Bianca innocently walked forth into the very jaws of death!

And not because she didn't see Mamelouk; because she *did* see him.

She was feeling bored. Her headache was better, and when she looked for Nils he had gone. Miss Bianca didn't particularly mind, she wasn't frightened, but all by herself she felt bored. If only she'd a book to read! — but she hadn't. The Head Jailer was practically illiterate, there was nothing to be borrowed from his shelves save one dog-eared pamphlet entitled *Cut Your Own Corns,* which Miss Bianca would have sooner died — O ominous phrase! — than look at.

She was bored, she had nothing to read: thus when a shadow fell across the entrance to the hole, she naturally put her head out.

About three feet away, big and black as a thundercloud, crouched Mamelouk.

This was the first time Miss Bianca had ever seen him

— Nils and Bernard being so careful to keep her out of his way — but she recognized him immediately from their description, and thought it a very unfair one. Indeed Mamelouk, except for color, was so like her old Persian friend, Miss Bianca was prejudiced in his favor at once. Nils and Bernard said he had a horrible leer; Miss Bianca thought it a rather nice smile. — It will be remembered, also, that though Mamelouk's tormenting of the prisoners, by leaping into their dungeons, was down in the Minutes in black and white, Miss Bianca had never been able to credit it, such was her misguided trust in feline chivalry. So she now looked out with no more than pleasurable excitement!

As for Mamelouk, his whiskers fairly twitched in anticipation. He'd suspected for weeks past that there was something of interest in that hole beside the stove; now he promised himself a proper mouse-tea — with a little game of cat-and-mouse first.

If only his prey could be lured from the safety of the hole!

"Little lady," purred Mamelouk suavely, "won't you come out and play with me?"

Miss Bianca advanced to the very threshold.

"Are you calling?" she asked hopefully.

"Certainly I'm calling!" purred Mamelouk.

"I'm sure it's very nice of you," said Miss Bianca; and to Mamelouk's surprise and joy tripped out into the room. "I should have been delighted to make your acquaintance sooner," she added, "but my friends are a little unsociable . . . How shall we play?"

"Like this!" grinned Mamelouk.

He flashed out a great black paw and touched her on the nape. Only a little more force, and he would have broken her back — as he intended to break her back; but only after reducing her to helpless terror. Such was his horrible nature.

"Now, run, little lady!" he ordered. "Run between my paws!"

"With pleasure," said Miss Bianca. She darted gracefully to and fro. "Touch, and touch again!" she cried. "What shall we do next?"

Mamelouk looked at her with renewed astonishment. She was the first mouse he had seen in years, for he had come to the Castle when only half grown — yet he couldn't believe his memory played him so false, that this was the usual way for a mouse to behave.

"A lady of spirit, I see!" he growled. "All the more sport, then, before the end! *This* is what we do next, my love!"

He flashed out his paw again and pinned Miss Bianca to the floor. She lay absolutely helpless, not an inch from his jaws, under a weight like a mattress stuffed with lead.

"What beautiful eyes you have!" observed Miss Bianca. "They remind me so much of a friend's . . . Were you ever in Persia?"

"No, I was not!" shouted Mamelouk. "And *this* is what

we do afterwards!" he shouted — with one movement scooping her up and flipping her through the air. From his point of view it was a mistake; Miss Bianca landed quite safe, if a little breathless, in the long hair of his back, where he couldn't immediately get at her. "Hide-and-seek!" cried Miss Bianca delightedly; and ran deeper in.

By this time Mamelouk was so baffled, and so angry, he would have made one mouthful of Miss Bianca there and then — if he could have got at her. But he couldn't. He rolled, and shook himself, then leaped and gallo-paded, but he couldn't shake Miss Bianca off. She nestled deep in his long thick coat, and clung on tighter and tighter, emitting little squeals of pleasure. ("I know it's a common taste," cried Miss Bianca, "but how I do enjoy a switchback!") It was Mamelouk who tired first, fling-ing himself down before the stove quite worn out.

Miss Bianca's voice next came from somewhere near the root of his tail.

"I'm sorry to tell you," she called kindly, "but your coat needs a *great deal* of attention. When were you last brushed?"

Mamelouk began to swear — using really the most dreadful language, but fortunately Miss Bianca couldn't quite hear. She just gathered that he was annoyed, and made haste to soothe him.

"Now don't get into a pet!" she begged. "I'm only speaking for your own good — "

"Cats aren't brushed!" shouted Mamelouk.

"Oh, indeed they are!" retorted Miss Bianca positively. "My friend often told me how uncomfortable it was, if his Page missed even one morning. — And what's this?" she cried, really distressed. "This dreadful matted patch?"

"Probably blood!" shouted Mamelouk. "Mouse blood!"

"No, it isn't," said Miss Bianca. "It's treacle. Really, what carelessness! — But at least I can get *that* out for you — if you'll only hold still."

Mamelouk held still. He was too exhausted to do anything else. Miss Bianca nibbled and nibbled, and at last nibbled the treacle patch clear. — But it wasn't *only* treacle: it was a tiny scrap of cloth, stuck with treacle to Mamelouk's fur! And with writing upon it!

"Do see about your brushing tomorrow," said Miss Bianca hastily. "Now forgive me if I run!"

Mamelouk had actually fallen asleep. Bernard and

Nils, rushing in at the sitting room door, could streak straight across to join Miss Bianca in their hole.

"Are you safe?" panted Bernard.

"Of course I'm safe," said Miss Bianca. "And just look at this!"

10

The Message

THEY had to scrape and scrape, and lick and lick till their tongues felt like emery paper, being careful all the time not to scrape or lick away any writing. (Mamelouk was right in one respect; the message, for such it was, was written in blood, from a pricked finger.) At last the treacle was cleaned off, and there quite clear upon the poor scrap of rag showed three or four words in an educated hand.

"And in Norwegian!" shouted Nils.

He pushed Bernard roughly aside, to see better. Bernard didn't mind.

"What does it say?" cried Miss Bianca.

They had never before seen Nils overcome by emotion. Now he actually used the precious rag to wipe his eyes! "For goodness' sake don't wash anything off!" cried Bernard — offering his own spotted handkerchief. "Just tell us what it says!"

Nils gulped and controlled himself.

"It says . . . well, roughly, it just says, *Shall I ever see Norway again* . . ."

For a moment, at these pathetic words, all fell silent. Then —

"But at least he's still alive!" exclaimed Miss Bianca.

It was wonderful what a difference the knowledge made. Each mouse felt a fresh surge of hope and energy. Discussing the matter among themselves — as they did for hours and hours — they decided that the prisoner must have prepared the message in advance, and seized an opportunity when Mamelouk jumped down into the dungeon to stick it to his fur. However despairing, then, the poor poet, besides being still alive, was still capable of resource! — and how much more should *they* be, at liberty at least within the Castle! "We've been idling!" cried Nils. "We haven't been using our heads!" This wasn't strictly fair, but both Bernard and Miss Bianca understood what he meant: while they didn't know the prisoner was *there* to be rescued, they had gradually let hopelessness get the better of them, and lived from day to day waiting on events . . .

"I shall explore the Castle more thoroughly," said Nils, wiping his eyes for the last time. "There must be *some* way out, besides the gate! I've just been sitting on the Ledge like a stuffed owl — "

"I shall make a timetable," said Bernard, "of exactly when the jailers go their rounds, and exactly when they unlock the dungeon corridor."

"And I," said Miss Bianca, "shall talk to Mamelouk."

The other two at once stopped making their own plans to argue with her. Even Nils now realized what risk she had just run, and as for Bernard, he could hardly trust himself to speak moderately.

"Don't think of it, Miss Bianca!" he begged. "Wonderfully as things have turned out, do please believe it's an even greater wonder you're not eaten up this minute! No mouse on earth could talk to Mamelouk *twice!* — and live to tell the tale! Why he *didn't* eat you — "

Miss Bianca looked down at her fan.

"I think I fascinate him," she said simply. "You may be perfectly right, perhaps he does mean to eat me — Oh, dear," sighed Miss Bianca in parenthesis, "how very different a nature, in that case, from my poor friend's! — but he *didn't,* you know. His expression, as I ran between his paws, was, really, quite fascinated. I'm sure he wants to meet me again — if only from dishonorable motives. Let me engage him in conversation, and guide it into the right channels, and what may I not learn, to our advantage? For if anyone knows everything that goes on in the Castle," said Miss Bianca, "it's Mamelouk."

Bernard and Nils couldn't deny it.

"But the danger — !" cried Bernard nonetheless.

"You and Nils make *your* plans," said Miss Bianca gently; "aren't they dangerous too? *You* have strength and agility; I — " she looked modestly down again — "have only charm. You must allow me to employ it. Now good night, dear friends, and in the morning to our tasks!"

She carried the prisoner's message to bed with her, and placed it tenderly under her pillow.

Before they all fell asleep, a short conversation took place in the room shared by Nils and Bernard.

"Nils," said Bernard.

"Um?" said Nils sleepily.

"Who called Miss Bianca a bit of a nuisance?"

There was a slight pause.

"I ought to be kicked," said Nils. "If you like you can come and kick me now."

"That's all right," said Bernard. "Good night!"

2

Now all was action and enthusiasm again. Nils and Bernard returned to exploring the Castle — Nils on the outside, Bernard within. (They left Miss Bianca alone as a matter of course.) Nils ran about the great walls, utilizing every nook and cranny, while Bernard even more daringly slipped to and fro at the jailers' heels, noting and memorizing their every movement. Miss Bianca deliberately threw herself in Mamelouk's way, and this was useful to the other two as well, since she kept him fixed in the sitting room for long periods at a time. Mamelouk couldn't tear himself away from her!

It is hard to speak too highly of Miss Bianca's courage — shot with vanity though it might be. Her gaiety and wit fascinated Mamelouk completely. At the same time, as she came to know him better, she recognized him to be just as cruel and wicked as Bernard said. He did indeed mean to eat her up! — He as good as told her so! "Can you really be as sweet as you look, little lady?" Mamelouk would purr, with horrible double meaning. "I wonder what's the way to find out?" Then it was always *just one more game,* or *one last game* — "To give me an appetite for my dinner!" purred Mamelouk. Miss Bianca's nerves were so taut, she had to go and lie down as soon as she regained the hole. — But she always did regain it: always, at the last moment, by some exquisite trick or clever piece of flattery, she held Mamelouk's paw suspended — and then skimmed like a hummingbird to safety.

Unluckily, when Mamelouk felt like conversation, it was mostly about himself, and Miss Bianca grew very tired of hearing what a handsome kitten he had been, and what an enormous sum the Head Jailer had paid for him, and how even dogs, in the days when he was out in the world, used to howl for mercy at the sight of him. (Besides all his other vices, he was a shocking liar.) One piece of information, however, she did gather, which she hoped might be highly important.

Every New Year's Eve, all the jailers in the Castle, including the Head, held a midnight feast. From midnight till dawn not a single one was on duty. "And not next morning neither," leered Mamelouk.

"Indeed? Why is that?" asked Miss Bianca.

"They've all got bilious attacks," leered Mamelouk, "they stuff themselves so! One's *supposed* to be on duty, the one who takes the prisoners their grub, but it's all he can do to stagger!"

Miss Bianca's heart beat with excitement, but she kept her wits.

"And do you have a bilious attack too?" she inquired solicitously.

"Not me!" swaggered Mamelouk. "I attend, of course, to prevent disappointment — and I eat everything going! — but the feast hasn't been spread yet that could upset my stomach! I am Mamelouk the Iron-tummed!"

But when Miss Bianca made her report to Nils and Bernard, she added that she was sure he was lying again!

"He protested too much," she explained. "I remember a child at one of the Boy's birthday parties who said the same sort of thing — until a footman carried him out! In *my* opinion, Mamelouk won't be on duty either."

"Which means," said Bernard eagerly, "that on *that* morning, the morning of New Year's Day — "

"We can get into the dungeon corridor!" shouted Nils. "All of us! *And* down through the grid — for a mouse can pass where a food pan can't! We may reach the prisoner at last!"

"But as to getting him *out,*" said Bernard, more soberly, "we're much where we were. A man can't pass where a mouse can; and even if he could, he'd still be inside the Castle. The gate won't open till next autumn; and we could never hide the prisoner until then."

"At least Nils can speak to him in Norwegian," said Miss Bianca, "and keep his spirits up. Nils can call a few words of Norwegian through each grid (like Blondel and Richard the First), and as soon as he gets an answer — "

"Down I'll jump!" promised Nils. "But in the meantime," he added, "how long *is* it, to New Year's Eve?"

Bernard ran out and looked at the Head Jailer's calendar.

"Three days," he reported back.

"In the meantime," said Nils stoutly, "I shall go on exploring."

They then passed a vote of thanks to Miss Bianca, and retired for the night.

None of them slept much, however, partly through excitement and partly because there was another thunderstorm. The thunderstorms at this time were more furious than ever. So was the River more furious than ever — lashing and beating between its banks like a captive dragon. Even up in their hole the mice could hear its voice, ever present between the thunder-claps, and almost more alarming in its steady, thwarted rage.

Yet the River was to prove their best, if erratic, friend.

3

Two days passed in feverish yet unrewarded activity. Bernard gave up making timetables and explored with Nils. They discovered several fresh cracks and crannies — what a buffeting the Castle had taken! — but none of any use to a man-size prisoner. Then at last, very early after the worst night of all —

"Come quick!" cried Nils, pulling the pillow off Bernard's head.

To Bernard's surprise, Nils had evidently been out already; his fur was damp and staring from the morning air.

"What, before breakfast?" mumbled Bernard. He was still only half awake.

"Bother breakfast!" cried Nils. "Come on!"

He was away before you could say knife, and now Bernard leaped up and followed. Together they ran recklessly across the sitting room, out into the corridor, up through the bars of the corridor window, and then down,

down, down the Castle walls to a little boss of rock out-jutting from the cliff itself. The last of the gale almost whipped them off their feet; below snarled the still angry River, tossing and turning in its bed.

"See anything different?" asked Nils excitedly.

Bernard leaned so far over, Nils had to hold him by the tail. He gazed with all his eyes. There *was* something different, though at first he couldn't make out what. Then he discerned at the very foot of the cliff, where once rock rose sheer from water, a great jumbled heap of stones.

"The Castle's crumbling!" cried Bernard.

"Not the Castle," corrected Nils, hauling him back. "*It's* too solid. But there was just one weak spot — as the River's found out! Look at those stones — *cut* stone! Look at those *steps!* D'you know what *I* think's down there?"

"Go on, tell me!" implored Bernard.

"An old water gate," said Nils. "Some time, down there, there's been a water gate. Stands to reason! No one ever built this castle just for a prison," said Nils positively. "In its time it must have been an honest Castle, *with* — stands to reason! — a water gate. Then it was blocked up; and now the River's worried it free again, like worrying the stopping out of a tooth. So there *is* another way out!"

For a moment they gave themselves up to happy excitement — Bernard congratulating Nils and slapping

him on the back, Nils flourishing his whiskers in honest self-approval. Then Bernard looked over the edge again.

"I wonder what part of the Castle it leads to?" he said practically. "And if it's unblocked all the way?"

"That we must find out," said Nils. "Come on!"

11

The Other Way Out

Down the cliff they scrambled again, down and down towards the river brink. It was a perilous journey, but they achieved it. (On some particularly difficult ledges they had to use each other's tails as mountaineers use ropes: one of them held on tight while the other slid down, then the one below made a back for the one above, or even caught him as he jumped.) Down they went and down — fur scraped, tails aching — and at last stood gasping but triumphant upon the heap of jumbled stone.

"What did I tell you?" panted Nils.

There was a water gate all right. Up under a cavernous stone arch — cut stone! — rose a flight of granite steps that disappeared into the gloom above, and in the buttress to one side was even an old iron mooring ring!

But how well had the River done its work? Were those steps still blocked, higher up?

Exhausted as they were, the mice had to know.

At least it was easier going up than coming down: though the steps would normally have been too high even for tail-work, the River, retreating, had washed down

ramps of sand and small stones against either wall. Nils
and Bernard slipped a bit on wet mud and shreds of
waterweed, but otherwise made good progress — and
with each step passed felt their hearts lift. It looked as
though the whole flight was clear! — As so indeed it
proved, right up to the top, where a high rusted gate
lolled half-fallen from its hinges . . .

Even a man could have squeezed by. Bernard and Nils
of course simply ran between the bars.

Where were they now?

"We're still pretty deep down in the Castle," said Bernard.

"Aye; at dungeon level!" said Nils.

Before them stretched a long narrow passage cut from
the rock itself. For a moment they thought it was the
corridor where the jailer with the food pans came to
let down the prisoners' food. But there were no grids in
its floor, the floor was solid rock too. (Nils and Bernard
ran up and down twice, to make sure.) So was one wall
solid rock. But in the other was a row of iron doors.

Dungeon doors . . .

"And there's another door, don't you see, at the *end*,"
cried Nils, "to bring the prisoners in by!"

At last it was clear, what the mice had never been
able to discover, how the prisoners were got into their
cells. (Small wonder, too, that the jailers weren't aware
of the River's work. Until a new prisoner arrived, they
had no reason to enter *this* corridor at all.) And as if to

confirm all speculation, at that very moment sounded a jailer's boots stamping overhead, accompanied by the clank of food pans. Nils and Bernard, by listening intently, could hear the grids creak up, one after the other, behind and above each iron door.

"All we need now," said Nils, *"is the key.* I see it all!" he exclaimed excitedly. "We get hold of the key — drop it through the grid — jump down ourselves — and all escape together by the water gate! All we need now is the right key!"

In Bernard's opinion this splendid plan had still a lot of loose ends. (How were they to *get* the key?) But he re frained from saying so. Indeed, it touched him to the heart to see Nils now run from sill to sill, attempting, in vain, to call beneath some Norwegian word of hope. The doors were set in solid rock, no voice of mouse could possibly penetrate. "Come on back, old fellow!" urged Bernard — not unsympathetically, just practically. "Now is the time, if there ever was one, for proper planning! Come on back to Miss Bianca, and let's *think!*"

It was a desperate, perilous journey again: first down the steps to the water gate, then up and up the cliff, and up again over the castle walls. Again, the dauntless mice achieved it. (Bernard was as dauntless as Sir John Hunt, and Nils as Sir Edmund Hillary.) The thought of all they had to tell Miss Bianca spurred them on, and though they ached in every limb, they never paused once until they reached the little boss of rock from which they had first peered down. There they allowed themselves a brief rest, while they got their breath (and also discussed whether to have a breakfast first and lunch immediately afterwards, or lunch straight away). Then off they set again. They had still a long way to go, but, as Bernard said, the worst was over.

He was wrong.

Fatigue made them careless. When at last they regained the door of the Head Jailer's sitting room, they hurried straight in without stopping to reconnoiter, and at that crucial moment, for the first time, met Mamelouk face to face. — Mamelouk was as surprised as they were, but he wasn't tired. For just one instant they all three stood transfixed — Bernard and Nils foolishly huddled together — then out flashed a cruel black paw and pinned them both to the ground!

2

At the same moment, Miss Bianca peeped out of the hole. She had been worrying all morning, ever since Bernard and Nils weren't there for breakfast. As the hours passed, her anxiety grew; all morning she had been running to the door to look for their return. Now at the sight that met her eyes she almost fainted! But she had got out of the habit of fainting, and instead uttered but one piercing shriek of dismay.

Mamelouk looked around. He grinned with pleasure. From his point of view, the appearance of Miss Bianca was the one thing needed to make the fun complete.

"So *these* are your unsociable friends?" he purred. "Now I shall have sport indeed! Would you like to see me eat them up?"

The three mice exchanged agonized glances. "Whatever you do, lie still!" adjured the glance of Miss Bianca. What Nils and Bernard had to convey was far more complicated: each longed with all his might, before he died, to pass on to Miss Bianca all their discoveries about the River and the water gate and the dungeon doors. It was obviously impossible. She saw only that they had *something* to convey, and of terrific importance!

"Ha, ha, ha!" laughed Mamelouk. "Come closer, little lady, and watch!"

He began to shake all over with cruel glee. (Nils and Bernard could feel it oozing from his very toes.) His grin stretched from ear to ear, revealing every one of his dreadfully sharp teeth, and even the wide red gullet behind; tears of mirth rolled down his whiskers and glistened in his fur like the spangles of a Demon King. Miss Bianca had never seen him so terrible as in this fiendish merriment — but she stepped bravely out towards him, summoning all her funds of wit, and resourcefulness, and feminine cunning.

"Which will you eat first?" inquired she. "You can't swallow both at once, you know!"

"Oh, can't I?" grinned Mamelouk. "You just watch me!"

"I meant, without spoiling your appetite for the midnight feast," explained Miss Bianca hastily. "It *is* tonight, isn't it?" she added. "The great feast when you eat more than anyone else, and everyone is so astonished at you? Dear me, they'll be astonished in a different way, if you're so full of Nils and Bernard you can't manage a bite!" said Miss Bianca, carelessly.

She was being very clever, both in disguising her true feelings and in thus playing on Mamelouk's vanity. It wouldn't be half so much fun for him to eat her friends before her eyes if she didn't seem to care about them, while his reputation as Mamelouk the Iron-tummed was his greatest pride. — He looked uneasily at the mice un-

der his paw. After their months of good living, both Nils
and Bernard had put on weight. Either one would have
made a square cat-meal, and in point of fact Mamelouk
was accustomed to eat nothing whatever all that day . . .

"Perhaps you're right," he admitted. "I'll just break
their necks and have 'em tomorrow."

"Dear me!" said Miss Bianca again. "I thought you
considered yourself quite a gourmet! My Persian friend,
whom I may have mentioned to you, always told me mice
shouldn't be hung even an *hour!* But I suppose you're
forced to live coarsely."

Mamelouk was stung.

"I don't live coarsely!" he shouted. "I live on the fat of
the land!"

"It's so nice to hear you take that view," said Miss
Bianca blandly. "It shows a truly humble nature. My
Persian friend, now — "

"Nor's my nature humble!" shouted Mamelouk.

" — my *Persian* friend," continued Miss Bianca, "had
quite a little witticism on the subject. 'Fresh-killed mouse,
caviar,' he used to say. 'One day old, ants' eggs!' Of course
if you don't *mind* eating ants' eggs — which at the Embassy we fed to goldfish — I've really no advice to give,"
said Miss Bianca kindly. "You must do just as you think
best."

Mamelouk was by now thoroughly confused. He didn't
want to spoil his appetite for the feast, he didn't want to
let Nils and Bernard go, and Miss Bianca had somehow

made it seem that if he killed and saved them up, he would be regarded as a goldfish! For a cat with two plump mice under his paw, the situation was really extraordinary.

The uncertainty in his mind began to transfer itself to his muscles. Very slightly, the grip of his paw slackened. Bernard and Nils looked at each other, hardly daring to hope.

"Or if I *might* make a suggestion," added Miss Bianca impulsively, "*do*, as you're dining out, pay a *little* attention to your coat. You might begin with your back."

"What's wrong with my back?" growled Mamelouk — confused afresh by this sudden change of subject.

"Just look!" said Miss Bianca.

Vain Mamelouk looked. Actually there was nothing wrong with his back coat at all, he'd groomed himself rather specially — but he couldn't help looking.

Over his shoulder.

Away from the mice.

"*Now!*" shrieked Miss Bianca.

With one instant's terrific effort Nils and Bernard wrenched themselves free and streaked like lightning for the hole. Miss Bianca skimmed in just ahead of them, and Mamelouk was left fuming outside . . .

3

Lunch was sausage and sauté potatoes, followed by treacle sponge, followed by cheese and biscuits. (Nils

and Bernard decided to cut breakfast after all and just
have twice as much of everything.) With so much to tell
Miss Bianca, they had to talk with their mouths full. She
for her part was alternately so enthralled by their discoveries, and so alarmed at the dangers they had run, she
could barely nibble a crumb.

"What heroism, and enterprise!" she murmured.
"Dear Bernard, dear Nils, how warmly I congratulate
you!"

"It is you who are the heroine," said Bernard soberly.
"Without your wonderful coolness and resource, we
should neither of us be here now."

"That's right," agreed Nils. "We'd be in Mamelouk's
famous tum!"

Miss Bianca shuddered.

"Pray don't speak of it!" she begged. "Or I really *shall* faint! Indeed," she added gravely, "we must now have no more thoughts of ourselves, or of anything else, until the prisoner is free. It is positively New Year's Day tomorrow, and how much still remains to be decided! How many obstacles loom still in our way! — Oh, dear," suddenly, uncontrollably wept Miss Bianca (a prey to delayed nervous shock, and no wonder), "that dreadful *dreadful* River!"

For a moment they all of them thought about the River.

"There we'll have to swim for it," said Nils hardily. "It's The Barrens on the other side," he added, "that bother *me* . . ."

For a moment they all thought about The Barrens.

"There we'll have to march for it," said Bernard.

Then they all thought about the prisoner, and their courage was renewed.

They began to plan in detail what had never been planned before — or, if planned, had never succeeded: the liberation of a prisoner from the Black Castle.

12

The Great Enterprise

Iᴛ was determined in the first place to act on New Year's Day. (Tomorrow.)

This really went without saying. New Year's morning, with the jailer on duty, also Mamelouk, too bilious to be efficient, offered the mice their one and only chance of entering the corridor above the dungeons.

"Or may we not assume it a certainty?" proposed Miss Bianca.

"Seconded," said Bernard.

For such a momentous discussion they were having an extra, special meeting of the Prisoners' Aid Society, Black Castle Branch. They just cleared lunch away first.

"Call it a certainty," said Nils.

"Carried unanimously," said Miss Bianca, from the Chair. "We all three, then," she proceeded, "enter the corridor — "

"Question," said Bernard. "*I* suggest Madam Chairwoman join us below at the water gate, thus bypassing at least some of the peril."

"I certainly *won't!*" cried Miss Bianca. "To venture

alone down to a River," she added, more formally, "without other members to assist and guide, is something no Chairwoman should be asked even to contemplate. We all enter the corridor *together*. Nils then makes contact with the prisoner — "

"Trust me for that!" shouted Nils.

"I'm sure we do," said Miss Bianca. "Nils next, through the grid, throws down the right key — "

She paused.

"How do we *get* the right key?" asked Miss Bianca.

"The jailer will have it on his belt," said Nils, "along with all the rest. Bernard and I have seen 'em. I throw down the whole bunch, and the prisoner will sort out which is his."

"But how do we get the keys from the jailer?" persisted Miss Bianca.

"By force," said Nils.

Miss Bianca had an uneasy feeling that the point wasn't really settled. How exactly *did* one use force on a jailer, if one happened to be a mouse? But she didn't want to undermine the meeting's confidence; also she recalled a saying of the great Duke of Wellington's, to the effect that whereas his enemies made plans of wire, *he* made *his* of string — that is, he always left something to the inspiration of the moment. Frail and pliable as string, yet in the end strong as a rope ladder, Miss Bianca trusted *their* plans might prove! — and passed on to the next step.

"Thank you, Nils," she said, "for your excellent idea. "You then jump down yourself — Oh, dear!" added Miss Bianca, now losing a trifle of her own confidence. "How do I get down?"

Nils and Bernard went into committee for a moment.

"I will jump second," reported Bernard, when they came out, "and between us we will stretch my handkerchief like firemen. Then you jump into it. It won't be half so dangerous as saving us from Mamelouk."

"I suppose I can," murmured Miss Bianca — and returned to her role as Madam Chairwoman. "Next, we induce the prisoner to place his confidence in us — "

"Trust me for that too!" shouted Nils.

" — and conduct him, he having unlocked his cell with the key provided, to the River bank. There have been far too many interruptions from the floor," added Madam Chairwoman Miss Bianca severely, "and I don't want to hear anyone say, 'Then we'll have to swim for it.' The Meeting knows it will have to swim for it."

"And then march for it," muttered Bernard.

"And then march for it," agreed Miss Bianca. (She ought really to have called Bernard to order too, but somehow she didn't.) "It thus appears," she continued, "that until the jailer goes his round tomorrow morning, there is nothing we can usefully do. Our best course is to get as much sleep as possible, in order to recruit our strength; though I must say I should like to leave things tidy!"

In fact, after sleeping all the rest of the day (while Mamelouk watched fruitlessly outside), they spring-cleaned half the night. There was no real reason for it, probably no mouse would ever take that hole again, yet Miss Bianca's instinct was right too: there is nothing like housework for calming the nerves. Mamelouk went off to the party shortly before twelve, so they could put all the furniture outside, then for hours all was peaceful domestic activity. Faintly, as Nils and Bernard took the carpet up, they heard the songs and shouts of the jailers' midnight feast; faintly, as Bernard and Nils cleaned the wallpaper with dry bread crumbs, they heard a last burst of merriment die away. As dawn broke, Miss Bianca, sweeping out a last pan of rubbish through the lobby, saw Mamelouk the Iron-tummed totter back and collapse before the hearth; by which time the nerves of all three mice were as calm as could be.

It was pleasant, too, as after a sustaining breakfast they took a last look round, to see everything so neat and clean.

"It wasn't such a bad hole after all," admitted Nils, as he got into his sea boots and buckled on his cutlass.

Cudgel in hand, Bernard nodded silently. He couldn't trust himself to speak. In spite of all the terrible circumstances, the hours he spent hanging wallpaper for Miss Bianca had been among the happiest of his life.

He was glad to hear *her* give the hole a kind word too.

"Adieu, dear hole!" murmured Miss Bianca softly. "Dear hole, adieu!"

Bernard picked up her valise. Nils looked out first, to see if the coast was clear. It was. Beside the stove, Mamelouk still snored and tossed in queasy dreams. For the last time, they picked their way among the cigar butts and the matchboxes and the chewing-gum wrappers. Miss Bianca cast a last compassionate glance towards the poor butterflies on the walls. But they were none of them sorry to see the last of the Head Jailer's sitting room.

2

Along the corridor they hurried, down some stairs, along a corridor and down more stairs again. It was all strange territory to Miss Bianca, but Nils and Bernard, after their explorations, ran on unhesitatingly. Not a soul besides themselves was about. Empty stretched the corridors, unguarded the stairs: all jailers save one, as Mamelouk had foretold, lay still abed, quite unable to lift head from pillow . . .

But where was that *one*?

As the mice approached the corridor above the dungeons, they began to take more care. At the last flight of steps Nils crept on in advance, while Bernard and Miss Bianca waited halfway down. "I hope he won't be long!" whispered Miss Bianca — for now that even their own footsteps were stilled the silence was frightening; the whole weight of the Castle seemed to press down on them like an enormous, million-times-magnified paw . . .

Then back Nils called in triumph, they hurried after, and beheld inert against an iron door — *holding it open,* like a doorstop — the jailer with the food pans!

He had got just so far before collapsing. The pans and their contents lay scattered all about. To Miss Bianca's extreme relief there was obviously no need to use force on him, for he was sound asleep.

What a moment that should have been! — What a *half*-moment, indeed, it was! But scarcely had the mice savored their triumph when they perceived something they hadn't bargained for.

There was no bunch of keys at the fat jailer's belt. The key ring dangled far out of reach overhead, where he had left it in the lock of the smooth, iron door.

No mouse can run up smooth iron.

"Now what do we do?" muttered Nils desperately.

"*Think!*" said Bernard. "We can't be beaten now!"

Enormous above them, like a mountain, loomed the bulk of the big fat jailer. — Like a mountain! Bernard had been mountaineering with Nils half the previous day; and the top of the jailer's head lolled only an inch below the lock . . .

"Stand ready to catch!" cried Bernard recklessly.

The Duke of Wellington would have been proud of him, as Bernard now acted on the inspiration of the moment. So was Miss Bianca proud of him, as Bernard with-

out the slightest hesitation leaped up onto the jailer's out-
stretched foot, and ran up his leg, and then across his big
heaving stomach — it heaved like an earthquake — and
then up onto his shoulder. "Oh, pray take care!" called
Miss Bianca — almost too far below to be heard! Bernard
waved back, and mountaineered on. Across the jailer's
face was a traverse to dismay the most expert; where
beard stubble gave place to bare flesh it was like travers-
ing polished rock. Bernard only just managed it — and
only just in time. The mountain turned volcano, as the
jailer sneezed; but Bernard, his foot at the roots of bushy
hair, had plenty to hang on to.

The jailer sneezed but in his sleep. Courageous Bernard plunged ever on, now as through a greasy jungle.
He attained the jailer's very scalp, and thence with a
supreme effort launched himself at the dangling keys
above. Twice and thrice he swung his full weight from
them; then out they came from the lock, and he and key
ring together cascaded jangling down!

"Over to you, Nils!" gasped Bernard.

Nils instantly ran on. (There was no time, now, for
praise or congratulations.) Bernard and Miss Bianca followed, dragging the keys between them. Beyond the
comatose jailer stretched the dungeon corridor itself;
with, set in its floor, at intervals of two or three yards,
the gratings over the dungeons. Nils ran swiftly from
one to the next, calling through each a word of Norwegian. The suspense was almost unbearable, for suppose

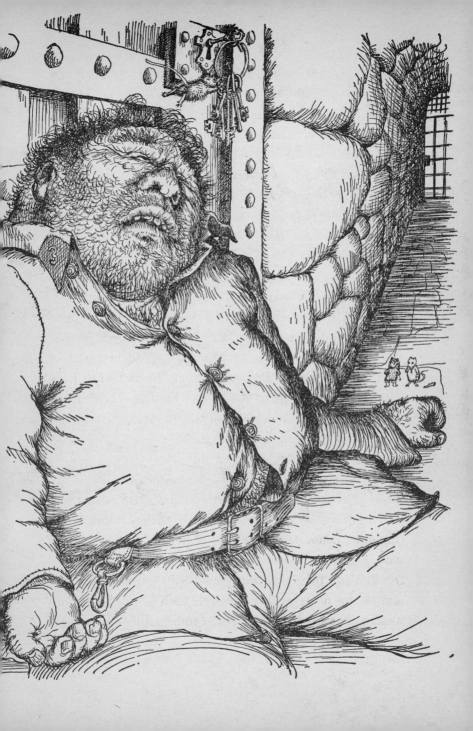

the jailer should really wake? An age seemed to pass before at the very last Nils halted. Had someone answered?
Evidently yes! "The keys!" cried Nils. Between them
they pushed the keys through the bars, easing them side
by side on the ring, then eased the ring through too, and
heard it fall below. "Norway forever!" cried Nils — and
unhesitatingly launched himself after.

So did Bernard. Miss Bianca, peering down, in a matter of seconds saw his handkerchief stretched to receive
her. Fortunately it was a very large handkerchief, more
like a young tablecloth, but even so she had to shut her
eyes before she could nerve herself to follow. Indeed,
only a joint cry of "Be brave, Miss Bianca!" gave her the
necessary impetus. But it did. She shut her eyes, and
jumped.

A moment later, they were all three together in the
Norwegian prisoner-poet's dungeon. The first stage of
the unachievable had been achieved.

3

But poor prisoner, poor poet!

It was difficult at first to tell whether he was old or
young, he looked so thin and ill and shaggy. The hair
that streamed in elflocks over the rags of a prison-uniform
— was it fair, or white? Were those eyelids red with age,
or with weeping? Huddled on the edge of his bunk, he
might have been twenty years old, or a hundred. Only

something in the *way* he huddled — elbows on knees, chin on fists — reminded Miss Bianca of the way the Boy used to huddle, if ever the Boy was terribly, terribly unhappy . . .

"Oh, he's *young!*" she whispered. "Poor, poor prisoner!"

What spoke most eloquently of his despair was that the bunch of keys lay still where it fell, on the ground beside his bed; he hadn't even stretched out a hand to see what it was. Or perhaps things had been thrown down at him before, in jailerish sport, just as Mamclouk sportively jumped down to spit at him . . .

For a moment the mice could only gaze in pity, while the eyes of Miss Bianca at least filled with tears. Then Nils again said something in Norwegian.

"Be still, my poor brain!" muttered the prisoner. "Is not one such delusion enough?"

In fact Nils had to repeat himself, shouting, about four times, before the prisoner looked wonderingly up. — First up, then around. Nils was almost hoarse before the prisoner looked *down.* As soon as they had his attention the three mice lined up, and Nils and Bernard took two steps back, then one forward, and politely pulled their whiskers. (There is nothing like sticking to manners, in any unusual situation.) Miss Bianca, in the middle, bowed.

After only the slightest pause, to get his legs properly under him, the prisoner rose and bowed back.

It must be remembered that he was a poet. It is the gift of all poets to find the commonplace astonishing, and the astonishing quite natural. The sight of Bernard and Nils and Miss Bianca — Nils in his sea boots, Bernard carrying a valise, and Miss Bianca wearing a silver chain — therefore didn't disconcert him in the least, and when Nils again addressed him in Norwegian, he was far more delighted than surprised.

— Yet how feeble his own poor voice, after the long silence of solitary confinement, as he courteously bade them welcome! Miss Bianca again felt her eyes prick with tears.

"Tell him we are come to save him!" she prompted.

"That's what I'm *trying* to," said Nils, rather impatiently. "But here goes again!"

He launched into quite a long speech, interrupted from time to time by questions from the prisoner.

"He just wants to ask after his relations!" translated Nils, more impatiently than ever.

"Tell him there'll be opportunities for that later," urged Bernard. "Tell him that just now we've got to hurry!"

By this time the prisoner, partly through weakness, partly to see his visitors better, had sunk down to his knees. Nils jumped onto his hand, and ran up his arm, and began to shout directly in his ear. ("I'm having to tell him all about the Prisoners' Aid Society!" Nils called down irritably.) Again an age seemed to pass before the

prisoner's expression turned from dreamy pleasure to as much as ordinary attention. But at last he began to understand, and his eyes grew brighter and brighter. He picked up the keys, and cradled them lovingly in his palm — bending on Bernard such a look of admiration that modest Bernard blushed; and at last, with a few brief words, rose shakily to his feet.

"What does he say now?" asked Bernard. "Will he come with us?"

"He says," translated Nils soberly, "that he puts his life in our hands."

The three mice looked at each other. They looked at

the prisoner's gaunt, feeble frame, and Nils and Bernard thought of the slippery steps down to the water gate, and of the angry River beyond. What a responsibility! But their courage was high, and so, it seemed, was the prisoner's. (He was a poet. He didn't think he was dreaming, as a prisoner who wasn't a poet might have done — and so missed his chance of escape.) Shakily but resolutely — his fingers trembling but his spirit firm — he tried one key after the other in the lock of his door . . .

At the third, it opened.

There is no more wonderful moment in life than when a prison door opens. It was not through weakness that the prisoner, for a moment, again sank to his knees. Then up he rose; only once shuddered, as the cold damp air whistled through his rags; followed the mice along the passage, and with a smile set his foot on the topmost of the water gate steps.

4

The River had lapped back; yet even as they descended, the roar of water sounded louder and louder in their ears. The River was angry still! But there was no help for it, they had to go on. Each step seemed a separate precipice, slippery with washed-up mud; the mice skidded and slipped, the prisoner had to brace himself for support against the wet, rough, rocky wall. In fear and trembling, yet all resolute, they descended. In fear and trembling they reached the bottom —

And there, wonder of wonders, beheld a raft hugging the bank for shelter, tied to the old iron ring in the old, newly revealed water gate wall!

"The luck of the mice!" cried Bernard. "The luck of the mice at last! — Nils, tell the prisoner to get on board! You, Miss Bianca, run along the rope, and Nils and I will follow!"

Nils said something in Norwegian. The prisoner nodded. He was at the very last step; only a yard separated him from the raft. Then that foot slipped, in he fell, a powerful undertow sucked him down, and the faithless River carried him away!

13

The Raft

WITHOUT an instant's hesitation, Nils and Bernard jumped in after. "Keep his chin up!" spluttered Bernard. "We must keep his chin up!"

"But where's he got to?" spluttered Nils.

At that moment, the poet rose to the surface; they struck out desperately towards him.

"Kick off your sea boots, you idiot!" choked Bernard to Nils; Nils kicked them off, and made better progress. But they couldn't help. The dead weight of the prisoner's head was too much for them.

"Swim! Swim for dear life!" shouted Nils in Norwegian. It was no use. The poet was too weak from his long imprisonment to manage more than half a stroke, and indeed by this time Nils and Bernard needed all their strength to keep going themselves. With a faint smile of gratitude — even in his extremity! — down the prisoner went for the second time . . .

Where was Miss Bianca, during these dreadful happenings?

She had done what everyone should do in an emergency; she had obeyed orders. She ran straight along the mooring rope and onto the raft. A woman came out of the reed house, but Miss Bianca didn't even notice her. She ran up onto an empty hencoop where she could see what was going on — and seeing, shrieked in dismay!

So did the woman shriek. The raft-woman took one look at Miss Bianca, and instantly kicked the hencoop overboard, right into the Norwegian poet's arms as he rose for the last time.

After that, for some moments, all was noise and confusion. The raft-wife shrieked again; out from the reed house rolled a couple of men, and between them they hauled the prisoner aboard — Nils and Bernard clinging to his clothes, and Miss Bianca clinging to the hencoop. All four were so full of water, the prisoner had to be lifesaved by the raft-men, while the mice lifesaved each other; but everyone was safe aboard!

2

All who use waterways, be it by sea, river or canal, speak essentially the same language. If each separate word isn't understood, at least the general drift is. The raft-people soon learned all they needed to — and besides were the very reverse of inquisitive. For instance, no one said anything about the Black Castle, though it loomed so directly above them; in the same discreet, almost off-hand way they supplied their guest with dry and anonymous clothing, and when he had changed made his old prison rags into a bundle, and weighted it with a flatiron, and sank it in the River. (The raft-wife also cut his hair for him.) And the moment the River had a little calmed, they unloosed the mooring rope and cast off.

"What splendid, kind people!" exclaimed Miss Bianca.

"Aye; proper seafarers," said Nils.

The mice made this last journey in the poet's pockets. He somehow explained to the raft-wife, when she wanted to chase them off, that they were friends of his. "Mind they don't run about loose, then!" warned the raft-wife grudgingly. (She had sacrificed her flatiron, but she couldn't abide mice.) So the poet put them one in each pocket — Bernard in the left, Miss Bianca in the right, and Nils over his heart.

From this snugness and security, each day, again, as on the wagon ride, they looked out upon a changing landscape. But now it was the *reverse* of the wagon ride: first they floated between cliffs on one side and The Barrens on the other, then through a country of bare heath and crooked firs, then through fat farmland, all tucked up for the winter but still very friendly and comfortable-looking. Here they sometimes passed wagons quite close to the bank, and then the three mice all leaned out and waved. (Miss Bianca once thought she saw Albert, but it may have been just a likeness.) The River, as though sorry for having nearly drowned them, behaved beautifully: it flowed with a strong, even current, just powerful enough to keep the raft floating steadily, but without sending so much as a ripple on deck. The raft-people told each other they had never known such fair weather! — and it made them all the kinder to the poet (though they would have been kind to him anyway), because they believed he was bringing them luck.

The poet grew stronger every day. Each day he ate three enormous meals of pork, fried potatoes, and apple jam. Some might have found this diet monotonous, but not the poet, after years of nothing but bread and treacle. — He always kept back three little portions for the mice, which they ate behind the hencoop, under his strict supervision on account of the raft-wife's prejudices. Then they had a short scamper and got back into his pockets.

Sometimes at night, because the moon was so beautiful, he let them run out again, just for a few minutes; and Miss Bianca was so inspired she wrote two new poems.

POEM BY MISS BIANCA, WRITTEN ON A RAFT

How beautiful the night!
    What silver ripples swim behind our wake!
All nature hushed, winds stilled, the waters calm,
    'Tis as we sailed upon an argent lake!

How beautiful the dawn!
    Aurora's fingers part the fading mist,
Sweet birds strike up their morning roundelays —
    'Tis as we sailed on seas of amethyst!

                  M. B.

The other was perhaps not quite so poetic, but even more heartfelt.

RAFT-SONG, BY MISS BIANCA

Day and night, between faraway banks,
    Smoothly glided a beautiful raft.
Sun and moon and the stars of the sky
    Look in blessing on cargo and craft!

Three brave Rafters with hearts of gold —
    Four poor Mariners saved from the foam —
Look down in blessing, sun, moon and stars,
    Carry them safely, swiftly home!

                  M. B

This one had a rather appropriate, watery rhythm; the three mice used to sing it each night, from pocket to pocket, while the poet slept.

Safely indeed, if not very swiftly, the raft bore them on. How glorious it was, to be headed for freedom at last! For their cargo was due at the Capital, and once there, said Nils confidently, the prisoner-poet, his strength now quite recruited, would be able to make his own way home.

"And I shall go with him," said Nils yearningly. "Ah, it'll be good to see Norway again, and take a glass of beer with the lads!"

Bernard looked at Miss Bianca. *He* was going home too; but where, oh where, was Miss Bianca's home? Would she disappear again into the world of high society — into her Porcelain Pagoda?

Miss Bianca was asking herself the same question.

14

The End

THE return of Bernard and Nils and Miss Bianca, their mission successfully accomplished, has been so often described in mouse history that only a brief account of it is now required.

Their welcome at the Moot-house was naturally tumultuous. The ceiling rang to shouts of "Three cheers for Miss Bianca!", "Three cheers for Bernard!", also "Up the Norwegians!" (led by Nils). Madam Chairwoman was actually observed to kiss the Secretary. The Secretary kissed Miss Bianca. All Bernard's relations kissed Bernard. Nils was presented with both the Jean Fromage Medal and the Tybalt Star — he'd in fact had one of these already, but swapped it for a mouth organ — and also, what he appreciated far more, with a replacement for every single possession lost with his sea boots.

Bernard and Miss Bianca made the list together, and they remembered everything: half a pair of socks, a box of Elastoplast, a double six of dominoes, a ball of twine and a folding corkscrew. When Nils saw them all neatly laid out on a silver tray, he showed emotion for the second time. As to the sea boots themselves, cobblers were working night and day on a new pair to his special measure.

It was more difficult to know how to reward the raft-people — until Miss Bianca recalled how the raft-wife had shrieked at the sight of her, and had made the poet carry them all in his pockets. Then a solemn declaration was drawn up, and signed and witnessed by Madam Chairwoman and the Secretary on behalf of all members,

to the effect that no mouse should ever in any circumstances set foot on the raft in question; and Bernard undertook to point it out, where it lay alongside the woodyard, to parties of not more than twenty at a time.

Miss Bianca's famous chart was richly framed and hung up beside the Aesop's fable picture over the speakers' platform. Below, a glass case enshrined her fan, Bernard's spotted handkerchief, and Nils's autograph, for the inspiration of future generations.

The Nils and Miss Bianca Medal, struck in pure silver, was awarded to Nils, Miss Bianca and Bernard. (Bernard himself quite agreed that "and Bernard" would have made it sound awkward. He had the most generous nature possible.) On one side was depicted the Black Castle, on the reverse a broken fetter. Particulars of this new award were at once distributed to every regional branch of the Prisoners' Aid Society, also to Societies overseas, with the request that it should rank above both the Jean Fromage Medal and the Tybalt Star.

"And we mustn't forget your mother's galoshes!" said Miss Bianca to Nils.

"You're right there," said Nils. "Ma promised she'd fair skin me, if I didn't bring 'em back!"

"Or would she prefer a new pair?" suggested Miss Bianca.

"Not Ma," said Nils positively. "Ma gets so attached to her old galoshes, you wouldn't believe."

So they went together to find them in the speedboat.

There it still lay, just as they had left it, gently a-rock on the Embassy boating water; and there were the galoshes too. Leaving Nils to look round, Miss Bianca took them into the cabin and filled each quite full of coffee sugar, and also wrote a grateful note of thanks on ship's writing paper.

When she came out again, Nils was still looking round. He was looking and looking, as though he couldn't bear to tear himself away.

"It *is* nice, isn't it?" said Miss Bianca.

Nils sighed.

"The neatest craft I ever saw!"

"So I think too," said Miss Bianca.

"A1 at Lloyd's!" sighed Nils. "I dare say the Owner," he added casually, "would have no use for a Nils and Miss Bianca Medal?"

"Now, really — !" began Miss Bianca. She was about to scold him quite severely, for she'd suspected all along that he took that splendid honor far too lightly. The wistfulness in his eyes, however, made her pause.

"As a swap," suggested Nils.

"In the first place," began Miss Bianca again, "decorations are never to be 'swapped' — " and again she broke off. If ever anyone wanted anything, badly, Nils wanted that speedboat. His hand, caressing a lever, quite shook with yearning! "And why not?" Miss Bianca asked herself. "I'm sure the Boy, if he knew all Nils's care of me on the voyage from Norway, would give it to him gladly!"

Aloud, she said impulsively, "Would you like the speedboat for your own, Nils?"

Nils was speechless with joy. He just pulled every lever in sight — turned on the headlights, rammed the quay, nearly swamped Miss Bianca, and reversed.

"But how will you get it home?" asked Miss Bianca, on second thought. "We know you mean to travel with the poet — "

"Far sooner under my own steam!" cried Nils.

"What, through all those dreadful oceans?" exclaimed Miss Bianca, aghast — and almost regretting her offer. "Please don't think of it, dear Nils!"

"Why, I can think of nothing else!" cried Nils. "Just hand me over the ship's papers, send a wire to Lloyd's telling them of the change of owners, and I shall be the happiest mouse alive!"

So Miss Bianca let him have his way. She felt he deserved it. — Also she felt she would never really understand Norwegians!

2

The farewell between the poet and his three rescuers was very touching. (As Nils had foretold, the poet made his own arrangements for getting home. He fell in with a Norwegian captain, with whom he was going to travel back to the port, and there sign on as supercargo, no questions asked.) The night before he left he met Bernard and Nils and Miss Bianca, by appointment, outside the Moot-house door.

"Little Miss Bianca," said he, stooping tenderly down, "as soon as I get back to Norway, I shall write a poem about you."

(Of course Nils had to translate.)

"Can I really deserve such honor?" exclaimed Miss Bianca modestly. "When all I did was but any mouse's duty? Yet I thank you from all my heart, and from all my heart wish you well."

With extreme delicacy, the poet but laid a finger, caressingly, on her head. Miss Bianca allowed her whiskers but to brush it. They still understood one another!

"As for you," continued the poet, to Bernard, "no stouter soul e'er breathed! I shall never forget your heroism, which it is quite beyond me to thank. And as for you," he added, to Nils, "all I can say is, look me up in Oslo, and we'll make a proper night of it!"

Then he tried to hug them all, which was manifestly impossible, and overcome by emotion turned hastily away.

"Farewell, dear poet!" called Miss Bianca.

"Farewell!" he called back over his shoulder. "Farewell, and God bless you all!"

Bernard and Miss Bianca then accompanied Nils to the Embassy boating water to see him off too. He couldn't take Miss Bianca's famous chart with him because it was already hanging in the Moot-house, but he assured them

he remembered the route backwards. ("Finest chart I ever set eyes on!" declared Nils.) Wearing his new sea boots, he stepped joyfully on board the speedboat; shook hands with Miss Bianca, slapped Bernard on the back, and with his usual cry (which we will not here repeat), blazed away, headlights flaring, towards the Mediterranean, the Bay of Biscay, and the North Sea.

Afterwards it all seemed very dark and quiet.

There was a long pause.

"And where shall *you* go, Miss Bianca?" asked Bernard in a low voice.

Miss Bianca hesitated. She was actually staying for the moment with Madam Chairwoman — who brought her breakfast in bed each morning, who couldn't spoil her enough! — but she obviously couldn't stay with Madam Chairwoman forever.

"Really I don't know," murmured Miss Bianca. "For the last six months, everything has been so extraordinary . . ."

"If the most devoted affection," began Bernard, "even though limited within a Pantry — "

At which moment he was interrupted by a loud voice from overhead.

"Why, if it isn't Miss Bianca!" cried the voice. "The Boy's Miss Bianca, that he's so a-fretting for! So she *was* left behind!"

A big hand reached down and scooped her up. Holding her carefully in his palm, one of the Embassy footmen was now displaying her to an Embassy housemaid. (They had met for a tender interview by the boating water.)

"Let alone the reward offered," added the footman, "I've always had a kindness for the Boy! — I'd be glad to send her back to him anyways! As it is, five golden guineas for us, and off by Bag she'll go — the little beauty!"

From that callous yet altruistic palm Miss Bianca looked down at Bernard.

"Did you hear?" she called softly.

"I heard," said Bernard.

"*Fretting for me!* Ah, it's not for my Porcelain Pagoda," called Miss Bianca, "that I quit you, dear Bernard! Pray believe me! It is but Fate, that casts our lots so far apart! I must return to the Boy!"

"I always thought you would," said Bernard bravely. "I always knew it, in my bones. Farewell, dear Miss Bianca!"

"Farewell, dearest Bernard!" called she.

The footman carried her into the Embassy. What a welcome there awaited her! Amid universal rejoicing cream cheese was at once set out in a silver bonbon dish; the new Ambassador offered one of his own silk handkerchiefs to furnish her with temporary sheets; and a place was immediately booked for her in the next Bag to Norway.

So ends the heroic tale of Bernard and Nils and Miss Bianca.

Nils, after innumerable adventures, reached Norway in safety; and met the poet again in Oslo, where they went out to dinner and the theater and supper afterwards. The poet kept his word and wrote a beautiful poem about Miss Bianca, which was printed in several anthologies.

Bernard became Secretary of the Prisoners' Aid Society, and had a useful, respected and happy career.

Miss Bianca, reunited with the Boy, and once again domiciled in her Porcelain Pagoda, was happy too. It was really the life that suited her best.

But they none of them ever forgot each other, or their famous adventures in the Black Castle.

THE END

MS READ-a-thon— a simple way to start youngsters reading

Boys and girls between 6 and 14 can join the MS READ-a-thon and help find a cure for Multiple Sclerosis by reading books. And they get two rewards — the enjoyment of reading, and the great feeling that comes from helping others.

Parents and educators: For complete information call your local MS chapter. Or mail the coupon below.

Kids can help, too!